It felt good to have Hannah beside him.

Maybe it felt a little too good, Jackson cautioned himself. He'd hoped that time would take a toll on her affections, if not on his. But all that three years had done was make her that much more beautiful to him, that much more stirring.

Her perfume drifted along the air, reminding him of how much he actually missed her.

All it would have taken was a trip back to set that longing to rest, and there were times when he had almost given in to the temptation.

But he hadn't.

He hadn't left Storkville in the first place just to come sneaking back. No matter how much he'd wanted to return. He'd left town back then for his own good. And hers....

* * * * *

Dear Reader,

Though August is already upon us, we've got yet another month of special 20th anniversary titles sure to prolong your summer reading pleasure.

STORKVILLE, USA, our newest in-line continuity, launches this month with Marie Ferrarella's *Those Matchmaking Babies*. In this four-book series, the discovery of twin babies abandoned on a day care center's doorstep leads to secrets being revealed…and unsuspecting townsfolk falling in love!

Judy Christenberry rounds up THE CIRCLE K SISTERS with *Cherish the Boss,* in which an old-school cowboy and a modern woman find themselves at odds—and irresistibly attracted to each other! In Cara Colter's memorable VIRGIN BRIDES offering, the "world's oldest living virgin" meets the man she hopes will be her *First Time, Forever.*

Valerie Parv's THE CARRAMER CROWN continues, as a woman long in love with Michel de Marigny poses as *The Prince's Bride-To-Be.* Arlene James delights with *In Want of a Wife,* the story of a self-made millionaire who is looking for a mother for his adopted daughter—and, could it be, a wife for himself? And Natalie Patrick offers the charming *His, Hers…Ours?,* in which a marriage-wary pair play parents and discover they like it—and each other—far too much.

Next month, look for another installment of STORKVILLE, USA, and the launch of THE CHANDLERS REQUEST…from *New York Times* bestselling author Kasey Michaels.

Happy Reading!

Mary-Theresa Hussey
Senior Editor

Please address questions and book requests to:
Silhouette Reader Service
U.S.: 3010 Walden Ave., P.O. Box 1325, Buffalo, NY 14269
Canadian: P.O. Box 609, Fort Erie, Ont. L2A 5X3

Those Matchmaking Babies

MARIE FERRARELLA

Silhouette
ROMANCE™
Published by Silhouette Books
America's Publisher of Contemporary Romance

Special thanks and acknowledgment are given to
Marie Ferrarella for her contribution to the
Storkville, USA series.

To Tina Colombo, with thanks and appreciation

SILHOUETTE BOOKS

ISBN 0-373-19462-5

THOSE MATCHMAKING BABIES

Visit Silhouette at www.eHarlequin.com

Printed in U.S.A.

STORKVILLE, USA

Storkville folks hardly remember the day
the town bore another name—because the
residents keep bearing bundles of joy! No
longer known for its safe neighborhoods and
idyllic landscape, Storkville is baby-bootie
capital of the world! We even have a legend
for the explosion of "uplets"—"When the
stork visits, he bestows many bouncing
bundles on those whose love is boundless!"
Of course, some—Gertie Anderson—still
insist a certain lemonade recipe, which
is "guaranteed" to help along prospective
mothers, is the real stork! But whether the
little darlings come from the cabbage patch
or the delivery room, Storkville folks never
underestimate the beauty of holding a
child—or the enchantment of first love
and the wonder of second chances....

Prologue

The babies were crying again.

Crying and sapping her strength bit by bit.

The buzzing in her head increased, fueling the desperation that was threatening to wash right over her.

She loved them, truly loved the babies. But she wanted to be free. Wanted once more to taste and touch the freedom of being responsible only for herself, not two small lives. Wanted the freedom of waking up in the morning after a long night's sleep, knowing that any decision she made that day would affect her and only her.

Freedom. It whispered enticingly to her, its song riding the waves of the wind.

She slouched behind the steering wheel of the ancient vehicle, driving slowly now through the streets of a town whimsically renamed Storkville, weighed down by the responsibility she shouldered alone. Yes, there was her sister to help, and to worry, but the bottom line was the babies were hers. Hers to raise, hers to feed. Hers to account for and to.

Tears welled up in her eyes as she bit her lower lip. She couldn't take it anymore. She was too young to feel this old, this hopeless, this hemmed in.

If only there was a way...

She saw the building then.

At first glance, it looked like a house lifted from another era, when things were simpler. When men who created babies stayed to see them grow to maturity rather than disavowing any connection to them, disappearing forever from their lives. A stately Victorian house, prim and proper in its appearance, yet somehow warm and inviting, like a maiden aunt who baked wonderful cookies.

She stared at it, slowing the old car even more.

The sign before the house proclaimed it to be a daycare center.

A daycare center in a town known for its love of babies. For its love of children of all ages.

She looked back at the two tiny infants with identical faces if not identical genders who sat strapped in their car seats behind her. Their cries had quieted, but the noise still echoed in her head. They would start again soon—the cries, the demands.

She sighed, looking at the building. In a moment, the daycare center would be behind her. Just like the rest of her life.

Her eyes widened as the idea came to her.

And suddenly, there was a way....

She sat up straight, no longer slouching, no longer hopeless.

She knew what she had to do.

Chapter One

"Hannah! Hannah, you've gotta come, like, quick!"

Standing in her front room, Hannah Brady's heart somersaulted into her throat. Those were not exactly the kind of words the owner of a newly established daycare center wanted to hear.

"Wait here." The unnecessary instruction was issued to the eighteen-month-old Hannah deposited into a wide playpen a second before she hurried to see what was going on.

The high-pitched entreaty had come from Penny Sue Lipton, her fifteen-year-old part-time volunteer. Stuck halfway between the childhood of her past and the inviting promise of the adulthood in her future, for Penny Sue, fifty percent of life was pure excitement, the other fifty percent was pure boredom. Hannah tried to calm herself with that knowledge as she rushed to the rear of the Victorian building she had inherited from her Great-Aunt Jane just at what had felt like the eleventh hour of her life.

But when she heard Gertie, who everyone knew as Aunt Gertie and who was well into her sixties and as stable as the day was long, call out, "Oh my dear lord, Hannah, come quickly. You're just not going to believe this," Hannah had a sinking feeling that this wasn't just Penny Sue overreacting. She had trouble.

As far as she knew, all the occupants of the daycare center, tiny and otherwise, were accounted for. That meant that none of them had gotten into any sort of mischief that would throw two of her volunteers into what amounted to a dither.

Reaching the back of the building Hannah discovered that none of her small charges were in trouble...but there certainly was trouble. Trouble with a capital T.

Hannah's mouth dropped open as she came to a skidding stop beside the two volunteers—and two babies, neither of whom she recognized. Aunt Gertie was holding one of the two infants in her arms, cooing to it to get it to stop its fussing. Penny Sue was squatting down beside her, scooping up the other child. The babies had on identical clothes and seemed to have emerged out of identical infant seats.

Penny Sue turned toward Hannah, grinning broadly. Her green eyes were dancing. What Penny Sue lacked in experience, she made up in enthusiasm. The young girl clearly loved babies.

The one she was holding had a firm grip on her curly, reddish hair. "Hey wow, like, isn't this cool, Hannah? They were like, there, on the doorstep when I opened the back door. Foundlings." She held the baby up a little higher, as if presenting it for show and tell. "Just like in those old movies."

Hannah had a feeling that, unlike in the old movies, the babies wouldn't go back to their rightful owner at the end of two hours, right before the second feature. She pressed her lips together.

"All we need is the sound of violins and snow falling. Speaking of which," she said, glancing out at the darkening sky with its smell of rain in the air, "we'd better get them inside before they get sick."

As the two women withdrew into the warm kitchen scented with freshly baked sugar cookies, courtesy of Aunt Gertie, Hannah grasped an infant seat with each hand and dragged both into the house. She placed the seats just inside the door, then picking up the lone diaper bag that had been beside the seats, she shut the door behind her.

And the morning had got off to such a good start, she thought. She'd gotten two new charges with the promise of three more next week. Business was picking up and it was beginning to look as if she was finally going to be able to compensate Gertie and Penny Sue for their time.

So much for that happy, satisfied feeling. She turned to look at Penny Sue, hoping against hope for answers. "Where did they come from?"

Smitten by the baby she was holding, Penny Sue didn't bother looking up. Instead, she lifted a shoulder haphazardly and let it drop. "Beats me."

Gertie, her own arms filled with baby, was standing closer to Hannah. Curious, Hannah ran the back of her hand against the baby's cheek. Bright blue eyes looked at her and the child cooed. There wasn't the hint of cold about the soft skin.

"Well, they weren't out there for long," Hannah judged. She looked at Penny Sue. "What made you open the door when you did?"

Very carefully, Penny Sue separated a thick strand of her hair from small, pudgy fingers. "I just walked into the kitchen—I smelled Aunt Gertie's cookies which were, like to die for." She flashed Gertie a grin, then saw Hannah's look urging her on. "And then I thought I heard somebody knock."

If someone knocked, that meant that someone had to have been there. Maybe just turning away when Penny Sue came to the door. Maybe the teenager had caught a glimpse of whoever had abandoned the children without realizing it.

"Did you see anyone?" Hannah's voice was eager.

Penny Sue shook her head. "I saw the babies first because they were making this noise, you know? And then I, like, called you to, like, come quick." Hannah tried not to look impatient. Penny Sue must have realized what she was doing because she said, "I know, I know, stop using the word *like*. I'm, like, trying—" Chagrined, she bit her lip. "I mean—"

Hannah held up her hand. This wasn't the time to play Professor Higgins to Penny Sue's Eliza Doolittle. "Right now, I just want to know if you saw who knocked on the door."

Suddenly, Penny Sue's eyes brightened. "Yeah, I did see someone. I saw some lady running off."

"What lady?" Hannah asked.

"I don't know. I never saw her before," Penny Sue

replied, looking at Hannah. "I mean, like, she was hurrying away and—"

Coming to Penny Sue's rescue, Gertie held up a crumpled piece of paper. "Hannah, look, there's a note. I just found it inside the baby's sweater."

Taking the yellow piece of paper from Gertie, Hannah looked at it. The edges were jagged and torn, as if it'd been hastily yanked off a pad or out of a notebook.

"What's it say, what's it say?" Penny Sue breathlessly demanded, coming closer to Hannah. Shifting the baby to her other side, she tried to peer over Hannah's shoulder to read it.

"Not much." Disappointed, Hannah read it out loud. "'I know you can take care of my babies better than I can.'"

The single line was written, not typed, which meant that this could have been an impulse abandonment, she reasoned.

Hand to the back of the baby's head, Gertie placed the infant against her shoulder, nodding thoughtfully as she looked at the yellow paper. "Must be someone from town if they know that," she speculated.

"Or they, like, said that to throw you off the trail," Penny Sue said excitedly. "Maybe these are kidnapped babies, or, like, maybe—"

Hannah sighed. She didn't need this. Trying to steer carefully through the narrow waters and sharp turns of the situation facing her, she dropped one hand onto Penny Sue's shoulder.

"Or, like, maybe," Hannah suggested fondly, a smile lifting the corners of her mouth, "we'd better call in Sheriff Malone before you get any more carried away.''

Sheriff Tucker Malone flipped closed the small spiral pad he'd been using to take down notes and tucked it into the pocket of his bomber jacket. He looked from Penny Sue to Hannah. ''And that's all any of you can tell me?''

Hannah exchanged looks with the young girl beside her. It was obvious that Penny Sue felt nervous, but Hannah knew it was the demeanor of the sheriff himself and not any secret she was hiding that made the teenager fidgety.

''That's all any of us know, Tucker,'' Hannah told him. ''Whoever left those babies looked like a stranger.''

''To Penny Sue,'' Tucker qualified, glancing at the young girl. It was obvious that he didn't set much store by anything Penny Sue had said.

''But I—'' Distressed, Penny Sue began to protest in defense of herself. Hannah gently cut her short.

''Why don't you go help Aunt Gertie with the children?'' she urged kindly. ''I'm sure she's got her hands full right about now. The afternoon snack is way overdue.''

''Sure thing, Hannah.''

Resolutely, Penny Sue nodded and withdrew from the formal living room where Hannah and Tucker were sitting opposite one another.

The babies were in their seats on the floor before them, waving their hands and kicking their feet—two pieces of animated evidence. Beside them were all the worldly things they appeared to have: a diaper bag with two feeding bottles, two chewed plush toys and a delicately ornate baby rattle that had all the appearance of being an heirloom. Hannah knew Tucker was hoping that the latter might be traceable, but he had expressed his doubts.

The babies were carbon copies of one another, with reddish-brown hair and large blue eyes. Each baby was wearing a sweater with a name embroidered on it: Steffie and Sammy. As to what their last name was, that was anyone's guess.

"One of each," Tucker murmured, looking down at the babies. He raised his eyes to Hannah. "Any thoughts on the matter?"

"Other than being stunned?" She shook her head. The babies had been all she'd thought about since she'd placed the call to the sheriff's office. "No."

Steely eyes held hers captive. Tucker always knew when he was being lied to, although he didn't see the reason for it now. "Any particular reason the mother picked you to leave them with?"

She didn't care for where this was going. "We don't know it's a mother," Hannah pointed out. "Just because Penny Sue saw a woman hurrying away in the distance—"

"True enough," he interrupted. "Know anyone who'd leave them with you?"

"If I knew the person who'd leave them, then I'd know the babies," Hannah pointed out. "And I don't." She looked down at the two round, shiny faces. "It's as much a mystery to me as it is you. That's why I called you."

And it was true. If she had known the troubled parent who had chosen to leave these adorable children with her, she would have done everything in her power to talk them out of it before ever bringing Tucker into the picture. Tucker Malone, as everyone knew, was a good man, an honest man, but he believed in adhering to the letter of the law and compassion was not among the qualities she would have attributed to him right off the bat.

Compassion, she felt, was what was needed here. For everyone involved.

"How about that anonymous donation you were supposed to have received when you opened the center? The one to help you keep things operating smoothly."

She looked at him sharply. "How did you know about that?"

He pushed his Stetson back on his head with his thumb. "Word gets around here, you know that, Hannah. Think that whoever gave you the donation did it for a reason?"

She didn't follow him. "Such as?"

"Such as a down payment on having you take the babies. Conscience money," he clarified.

She looked at the babies, stunned by the thought. "No." She found her voice and it grew stronger. "I don't believe that."

"Just a thought." Tucker rose, careful to sidestep the infant seat. "Well, I'll see what I can do about this." He picked up the rattle from the sofa, slipping it into his front pocket as well. "In the meantime, we're not really set up for this kind of thing." He looked at Hannah, who had stood up next to him. "Why don't I get Health and Human Services to appoint you temporary guardian of these two until I can find something more to go on? After all, you're a licensed foster parent.''

Caught off guard, Hannah looked down at the twins. She hadn't really thought much beyond reporting the incident to the sheriff. Being responsible for the children on a twenty-four-hour basis was something she hadn't even considered, despite being a certified daycare administrator.

''You mean keep them?''

''Not keep them,'' he amended. ''Just have them on loan. They wouldn't look too good in the county jail and I don't have any place else to put them. What better place for them than in a daycare center?''

Pointing out that the key part of the word was *day* seemed somehow futile from where she was standing. Reluctantly, she had to admit that Tucker was right. Where else could the babies go?

Besides, in the last half hour, waiting for Tucker to arrive, Hannah had found herself already falling in love with the small foundlings.

There was no point in putting up an argument. ''Okay, I guess you're right.''

Tucker nodded. ''I'm the sheriff, I'm supposed to be.'' He pulled the brim of his hat down and turned toward the doorway. One of the babies began to fuss. ''I'll see myself out.'' Pausing at the threshold, he told her, ''I'll let you know if I find out anything.'' Tucker's eyes met hers just before he left. ''You do the same.''

Hannah stooped to pick up the fussing baby. Holding Sammy against her shoulder, she patted his small back. ''Count on it.''

* * *

She'd been torn about the next step, knowing it had to be taken, yet hesitating to take it. Not because of any doubts in her mind as to the competence of the man she was about to call, but because of doubts Hannah had as to her own reaction. Her own ability to stoically withstand a meeting face-to-face, with him. With Jackson.

But there was no getting around it. The babies had to be checked out by a competent pediatrician. Storkville now had one. Five months ago, because of his own failing health, Dr. Gregory Bowen had retired after practicing in Storkville for thirty years. Four months ago, Dr. Jackson Caldwell, Jr., newly returned to town to bury his father, Jackson Sr., took over Dr. Bowen's practice.

It had taken Jackson very little time to reclaim his place in the community he'd abruptly left behind three years ago. After a while, it was as if he had never really left.

Hannah hesitated calling him because she was afraid that the same thing would happen with the place Jackson had once occupied in her heart. A secret place she had never told anyone about. Especially since she'd married his best friend.

But she'd placed the call, knowing that there was no other choice open to her, telling herself that she was an adult now and it was time for her to behave like one. At least outwardly.

After four months of waltzing around and carefully avoiding him, she'd invited Jackson into her home and stood now silently watching him as he examined the babies in one of her late great aunt's guest rooms.

It was a bedroom out of another era, when ladies' bedrooms were more feminine and ladies themselves held their tongues rather than let their true feelings be known.

Maybe things hadn't changed all that much after all, she thought, waiting for his prognosis.

She hadn't had a chance to redecorate the bedroom. There'd been so much to do with preparing to open the new daycare center that all she'd had time to do was air the room out. She wished she'd picked the living room for the exam to take place in, instead of here. With the sky dark and pregnant with fat rain clouds just outside the window, it felt as if there were ghosts looming inside the room. Not the least of which were ghosts from her own past, a past she'd wanted but had never really had with Jackson.

Jackson returned his stethoscope to his neck and smiled at a twin. Sammy looked as if he returned the smile, his eyes crinkling. Jackson was slower raising his eyes to Hannah.

"Except for Steffie's runny nose and sniffles, both babies appear to be in perfect health. Whoever left them on your doorstep certainly didn't abuse them."

"Other than depriving them of love and dumping them on a stranger's doorstep." Hannah bit back the bitterness she knew he could hear in her voice.

Moving to the side, she busied herself with slipping a fresh diaper on Sammy and deliberately avoided looking at Jackson.

Slowly, he slipped the stethoscope into his bag. He'd been surprised, to say the least, to get the call from Hannah this afternoon. He'd also been more pleased than he'd wanted to be to hear her voice on the other end of the line. He'd been back for over four months now and had only managed to catch fleeting glimpses of her in and around town.

He was avoiding her as much as she was avoiding him, he supposed.

But bumping into one another had been inevitable. After all, the town was not all that large. Jackson just hadn't expected their first meeting after so long to be this dramatic.

In his heart, he supposed he was relieved he hadn't been called out to examine one of Hannah's own children. A child created out of her and Ethan's love. It had surprised him to learn that Ethan and Hannah had had no children. But then, they had only been married a little more than two years before Ethan had died in that car crash.

That, he recalled, had been over a year ago.

Jackson glanced at Hannah. How had she handled the pain of Ethan's death, and did she still love her late husband?

With effort, he blocked out the thought, pushing it away. He had no business wondering about that. No business being anything but a pediatrician. And perhaps, if she'd still have him, Hannah's friend. Present or absent, he'd always been Hannah's friend. And never more of one than when he had left town.

The silence was making Hannah crazy. She grasped at the first half thought that crossed her mind. ''It was good of you to come.''

Goodness, did that sound as hopelessly stilted to him as it did to her? But what do you say to a man you once loved with all your heart, a man who'd never loved you at all? Who had gone out of his way to urge you into the arms of his best friend just to be rid of you? Or so it had seemed at the time.

She'd thought once that they were friends, and hoped for more. She'd come away with far less and learned a valuable lesson as well. Never bet your heart on anything but a sure thing. Neither Jackson, nor Ethan, it eventually became apparent to her, had been a sure thing.

She raised her eyes to Jackson's. "I would have gone to your office, you know." She'd expected to do that when she called for the appointment. Getting him on the line, instead of his nurse, had caused her to falter and act like a fourth-grade schoolgirl, forgetting her lines in the school play.

"It would have been far too much for you to handle," he told her, snapping his medical bag shut. "And you obviously had a lot to deal with."

Jackson knew he should go. But he couldn't quite make his feet take the steps that would lead him from the room and to the stairs. There were questions knocking around in his mind, questions that were begetting more questions even as he stood here.

So instead of leaving, Jackson looked around, seeing far more than the lacy room they were in. "It's a nice place."

"My great-aunt left it to me when she died. It has, as they say, possibilities," she said, pride evident in her voice.

It was the first time since he'd entered the house that he'd seen her smile. It took him back over years of memories he hardly admitted to himself he had. "Why a daycare center?"

It seemed so natural to her, she was surprised that he'd ask. "I've always loved children."

"Yeah, me too."

She laughed softly, unaware of the sound. "I've noticed." With Steffie already in her arms, she moved to pick up Sammy. "I'll take these two," she murmured. Then seeing the bemused expression on his face she added, "They're small."

"Not that small," he countered. Putting down his bag, he took Sammy from her. "Here, let me help. You can't do everything yourself, you know."

Her eyes held his for just a fleeting moment. She told herself that she felt nothing, that her stomach tightened only because it was trying to remind her that she'd had nothing to eat except one of Aunt Gertie's sugar cookies since the babies had turned up on her doorstep. "Why not? I have until now."

She was a strong, resilient woman. Funny, he didn't remember her being this resilient. With the bag in one hand, holding Sammy against him with the other, he led the way out of the room. "You've done well for yourself. Ethan would have been very proud of you."

Hannah followed him out.

She sincerely doubted that.

Chapter Two

"So, how are they, handsome?"

Caught off guard, Jackson discovered that Aunt Gertie was standing right outside the bedroom door. Knowing the woman the way he did, he realized he shouldn't have been surprised by her appearance. Hannah had left her downstairs to handle the parents who were coming to collect their children at the end of the day. He should have known she would be here the moment her job was completed.

The woman was the picture of eagerness as she looked at him over the rim of her glasses now, waiting for an answer. The tension he'd felt the moment he'd entered Hannah's new home lifted as he grinned at Gertie. "They're fine, although Steffie seems to be getting over a cold."

"Small wonder, being left out on a doorstep like that," Gertie said. Without waiting for an invitation, she took Sammy from Jackson, tucking the baby against her. Her countenance radiated warmth as she looked down at the small face. "Poor lamb," she cooed.

His sentiments exactly, Jackson thought. The situation still struck him as highly unusual. Child abandonment was something that you expected to hear about taking place in large cities, where, fairly or not, the citizens were thought to be colder, prone toward being disinterested even in their own children. The same sentiments seemed inconceivable here in a town known for its love of children.

Bemused, he turned to Hannah. "And you have no idea who left these babies on your doorstep?"

Hannah shook her head. "None whatsoever."

She had a feeling she was going to be saying that a lot in the next few days. Storkville was not the most exciting town on the map, and any deviation from the norm instantly turned into a source of entertainment and provided the populace with the opportunity to speculate to their heart's content. Given that the town was more or less two thousand strong, that could translate into a great deal of speculation.

"You know," Aunt Gertie murmured thoughtfully, still looking at Sammy's face, "in this light, Sammy kind of looks like you, Jackson. It's almost spooky. There was a photograph on your mother's dresser that looked just like this."

His curiosity piqued, Jackson leaned over Gertie's shoulder and studied the small, sleeping face. He didn't really see it. "You think so?"

Hannah's eyes darted to the other baby, then fleetingly passed over Jackson's face. She saw nothing more than Gertie's very active imagination at work.

"All babies tend to look like someone's baby pictures," Hannah said dismissively, hoping to put an end to that particular tempest in a teapot before it began. "I'm surprised at you, Gertie. Being practically the town's resident baby-sitter, you above all people should know that."

Gertie pursed her lips together, studying Sammy. The baby stirred, the pucker disappearing. The resemblance faded.

"Yes, I suppose you're right." Gertie raised her eyes to Jackson's. "If these babies *were* Jackson's, I know he'd do the right thing and step forward, marrying the babies' momma. Wouldn't you, Jackson?"

It suddenly dawned on Jackson what the older woman had to be thinking. As if this wasn't enough of a mystery to deal with, Gertie was tossing in another curve. He could just hear the rumors starting now: *Storkville's Dr. Caldwell providing his own patients.* He had to nip this in the bud, now.

"Don't look at me with those eyes of yours, Gertie." He glanced at Hannah. Did she share Gertie's suspicions? "I was nowhere near Storkville when those babies were conceived."

"What makes you think they're Storkville babies?" Gertie challenged. "Hannah thinks they were left by someone just passing through, don't you, Hannah?"

Curious, Jackson looked at Hannah for an explanation. *Did* she think the babies might be his?

Uncomfortable with the penetrating look she saw in Jackson's eyes, she looked away, her attention seemingly taken by the baby in her arms.

"Makes sense. The town's not that big. We know

everyone by sight if not by name. Nobody we know had twins ten, twelve months ago. It's not the kind of thing you can hide around here.''

There were times when your life was almost painfully an open book, she thought. Like hers had been with Ethan. The funny thing was, she'd been the last to know. Everyone except for her, she had the feeling, had known about her husband's roving ways almost from the start.

And then again, maybe she had just chosen to be blind, she thought.

''Maybe it's someone who left town,'' Jackson suggested.

Gertie looked at him beneath hooded eyes, her mouth amused. ''Which brings us back to you.''

''This seems to be where I came in.'' Jackson began rolling down his sleeves, then buttoned them. ''So I think I'd better leave.'' He looked at Hannah. ''I'll stop by tomorrow after my hours to see how Steffie's cold is doing.''

Like her brother, Steffie was sleeping. Was it her imagination, or did Steffie's breathing sound just a tad labored? Feeling a little uncertain, Hannah looked at Jackson. ''So you don't think I need a prescription or anything?''

He knew that look. It was the panicky one new mothers got the first time their baby was sick. He was surprised at the depth of Hannah's concern, but then, he shouldn't have been, he thought. He'd always known how big her heart was.

He tried to sound as assuring as he could. ''Not that I can see. These things clear themselves up. If you have any questions, just call. I'm staying at the house until I figure out what to do with it.''

Hannah noticed that Jackson had said "house," not "home" and wondered if that was telling or just a thoughtless slip on his part.

Gertie snorted again and they both looked in her direction.

"I'll tell you what to do with it, Jackson.'' Her eyes slid over Hannah before continuing, her implication clear. "You can marry yourself a good woman, have her redecorate the place and then have yourself lots of babies, that's what you can do with it.''

Handsome to a fault, the way his father had been before him, Jackson'd had had an endless parade of people try to match him up ever since he'd passed through puberty. He took Gertie's heavy-handed suggestion in stride.

"I have lots of babies,'' he pointed out to her, humor curving his generous mouth. "They troop into my office eight hours a day.'' He glanced at the baby she was holding. "Sometimes longer.''

One of Gertie's gray brows rose as she gave the man whose bottom she'd diapered more than once a penetrating look. "Of your own, doctor-boy, of your own.''

Jackson said nothing, though the smile on his lips became a little less animated, a little more forced. There would never be any babies of his own, because there would never be a wife in his life. There was no way he would ever risk making a mistake like that, the mistake of following his heart and ignoring his mind. Ignoring reality. Unlike his father, to Jackson marriage was not an institution he was going to defile by making a mockery of it.

More than that, he would never hurt the heart of someone who loved him. Of someone he loved…

He looked at Hannah and abruptly tabled his thoughts. There was no reason to allow them flow in that direction. The best way to handle futile situations was to avoid them, not explore them.

"Maybe someday," he said to Gertie, knowing that was the safest response he could make.

Any attempt at the truth, or even alluding to the fact that he intended to remain alone for the remainder of his life, would only get Gertie going. It would be tantamount to waving a proverbial red flag in front of a bull. Gertie took full credit for beginning the movement that had had the town council rechristening the town with its unusual moniker. It had all come about because of a rash of births that took place nine months after a blanketing power failure had hit the entire area. Even before that, Gertie had always behaved as if it were her preordained duty to couple together all the unattached citizens of Storkville. She'd tried her hand with him once or twice with no luck. He'd hoped that in his self-imposed exile she might have mellowed, but he should have known better. Leopards didn't change their spots and Gertie, if anything, had only gotten more determined with each year that passed by.

"Someday you'll be pushing up daisies, doctor-boy. The time to look to your future is now, in the present," Gertie commented.

He finished buttoning his second sleeve. "I'll keep that in mind."

"Why don't I see about settling these two in?" As easily as she had taken the first baby, Gertie now commandeered the second one from Hannah. Her eyes moved from Jackson to Hannah. "You can see Jackson to the door."

He was already on the head of the stairs, hoping to forge a path of retreat. "I know where the door is, Gertie. I came through it."

Hannah slipped her arm through his before she realized what she was doing, the gesture coming naturally to her from a time when she hadn't had to rethink every move, reexamine every word in order not to give away any clues to her actual feelings. For a second, she thought of pulling it away again, but that would only call more attention to the situation than she wanted. So she made the best of it, pretending that they were still at a point in time when there was so much of life in front of them, so much promise for them. Before she had become disillusioned by both Jackson and Ethan.

"Let's go while the getting's good," she urged him in a conspiratorial whisper, "before she launches into another full-scale assault."

"I think you might be right," he whispered back. Fascinated, he watched as his breath ruffled the stray hair along her temple. His stomach tightened.

It felt good to have Hannah beside him, her arm linked with his as they walked down the stairs.

Maybe it felt a little too good, he cautioned himself. He'd hoped that time would take a toll, on her if not on his affections. But all three years had done was make her that much more beautiful to him, that much more stirring.

Her perfume drifted along the air, just the faintest scent that aroused him and caused fragments of memories to dance through his mind, reminding him of how much he actually had missed her. Missed her even though she had lingered on his mind like a lyric that was just out of reach, a melody that refused to solidify itself into a full chorus. All it would have taken was a trip back to set that longing to rest, and there were times when he had almost given in to the temptation.

But he hadn't.

He hadn't left Storkville in the first place just to come sneaking back. No matter how much he'd wanted to return. He'd left town back then for his own good. And hers. And Ethan's if he thought about it, although to be honest, Ethan had not figured into the mix very prominently for Jackson. Other than Ethan being the better man for Hannah than he was.

Reaching the bottom of the stairs, he turned to say good-bye. The words wouldn't form into audible sounds. He just wanted to look at her. So they stood in the foyer, the hurricane lamp on the nearly table dimly outlining their bodies, throwing silhouettes onto the wall that were freer to move than they were.

She was more beautiful than ever, he thought again. The young girl he'd loved and had kept locked away in his heart had blossomed into a hauntingly beautiful woman in the years he had been away. But there was a sadness in her eyes that the smile on her lips couldn't negate or erase.

It made him ache just to look at her. And he wondered how he'd managed to stay away as long as he had. Stayed away even when he should have returned, if only as a sign of respect.

He owed her an apology, if not an explanation. Before he knew what he was doing, he took her hands in his. "I'm sorry I didn't come back for Ethan's funeral."

She lifted a slender shoulder, letting the incident, and the apology carelessly pass. She'd looked for him that day, and called herself weak for it.

"That's all right, there was really nothing you could do anyway."

Nothing but hold me, let me talk to you the way I used to. Did you know that all I wanted from Ethan for my first anniversary was a divorce? That I used to pray you'd come back to rescue me from the mistake I'd made. The mistake you encouraged me to make? No, I guess you wouldn't know that. You had your life and it was one you'd chosen to live—without me, she thought.

His hands tightened on hers, encasing them. He had the oddest feeling that he'd failed her somehow, that she'd needed him and he hadn't been there. "Hannah, what is it?"

Rousing herself, she squared her shoulders. Her look was studied innocence. "What's what?"

"There was something in your eyes just then—"

He'd been her friend once. Her friend always, in reality. And sometimes friends had to be cruel instead of kind. But the look he had seen just now undid him, melting away all his noble intentions and making him want to just hold her in his arms until whatever it was that bothered her passed.

"Just the lighting," she passed off with a laugh.

She drew her hands away, breaking the link between them. Hannah gestured around. "The house looks a great deal darker than it should in the evening. Great-Aunt Jane never had enough lamps or light fixtures in this place. It's something I'm planning on fixing, once I get a little ahead."

She was babbling, she realized and forced herself to stop. But he made her uncomfortable. Her *feelings* for him made her uncomfortable.

Her words had him reaching for his jacket and the checkbook in his pocket. Money, at least, had never been a problem in his life. If he couldn't give her what he wanted, at least he could help in this minor way. "How much do you need?"

"Oh, I don't know, maybe—" Hannah stopped abruptly when she realized what he was up to. Her hand covered his as if she were keeping him from drawing a weapon. "I'm not going to start that."

He looked at her, puzzled. When she kept her hand on his, he stopped trying to get his checkbook out. "Start what?"

"Taking money from my friends."

She'd always been headstrong, he thought. Apparently some things hadn't changed. "Don't call it taking, call it borrowing."

But she still shook her head. "It wouldn't matter if I called it Jacob, it would still amount to the same thing." There was no way she was going to take his charity. "I made it this far on my own, I intend to make it the rest of the way on the same path." And then she paused, debating, searching his face for her answer. "Several weeks ago, someone sent me an anonymous donation to help get the center started. That wasn't you, was it?''

This was the first he'd heard of it. ''No, it wasn't me.'' Although he wished it was. He'd known people with far more than Hannah who would have welcomed a no-strings loan. He let his hand drop. Only then did she withdraw hers.

Jackson smiled. He couldn't help the admiration that came into his voice. ''I don't remember you being this rigid.''

''People change.''

He shook his head again. What was that line, the more things changed, the more they stayed the same? ''Not you, Hannah, not ever you. You started out being sweeter than honey and you'll go on that way.''

She would have believed him once, believed he meant what he said. Now she merely shrugged it off. After glancing out the wndow, she looked at him. ''Well, I'd better not keep you. It looks like a nasty storm is coming. I wouldn't want to see you caught in it. The creek still has a habit of overflowing at the worst possible times.''

Was she nervous? Why? It couldn't be because of him. He'd never made her nervous before. He smiled at her words. ''Is there a good time for the creek to overflow?''

''Don't get smart—although you always were the smart one. Ethan always used to say that.''

He looked at her for a long moment. ''The smart one, huh?'' From where he was standing, he wasn't the smart one at all. ''Oh, I don't know about that.'' The wind, making its displeasure known, began to howl. He knew he really had to be leaving. "I'd better go. It was great seeing you again."

She let the smile come then. Unguarded. "It was nice seeing you, too."

Impulse prompted the words that came next. He spoke before he could stop himself. "Listen, maybe if you're not doing anything later this week—"

Self-preservation leaped up within her, bringing another quip to her lips. "I'll be doing a lot of things."

He took it as a rebuff, one he knew he deserved. It was better this way, he told himself. "Right. Sure. Well, I'll stop by to look in on Steffie. You—"

Jackson moved to pick up his medical bag and froze. He had no idea if it was the lighting in the foyer, or if it was seeing her after so many years of just thinking about her. His hands found their way to her hair, framing her face a second before his lips touched hers.

He told himself that what he was doing was meant in friendship, but he was a lousy liar, especially when it came to himself.

He kissed her because he needed to, because he wanted to and because he couldn't find enough strength to walk away from the moment and the temptation. The light had fallen along her lips and all he wanted to do was seal it in permanently while sampling a taste. Just a single taste. Just this one time.

Her breath evaporated a second before she felt the pressure of his mouth on hers. The exact second when she realized what he was about to do.

She'd kissed him once before, at her twenty-first birthday party. They'd both been a little bit intoxicated, and a little less inhibited. He'd kissed her in the garden while they had made a wish on a firefly, thinking it was a shooting star falling to earth.

The power of that kiss had remained indelibly marked on her soul all these years.

It paled now in comparison and fell silently away in the wake of this one.

Her head began to spin wildly. It felt as if she had consumed an entire bottle of wine in a few seconds on an empty stomach. The force of his kiss rushed through her. He was being gentle: as gentle as snowflakes at the beginning of the season's first snowfall.

The impact was all the greater for it.

She would have said that as gentle as it was, there was a wealth of passion in his kiss. But how could the man be passionate when he'd removed himself so entirely from her life? When he hadn't taken the trouble to even come to see her after he returned to town?

It made no sense at all.

But it was hard to make sense when lightning was igniting her whole body. When the stillness around her only magnified the sound of her pounding heart.

She had been waiting ten years for him to kiss her again.

There were some things that time, with its misty powers, enhanced, playing a mischievous trick that made you believe that something was actually better than it had been. But time had played no such tricks here. If anything, time had muted the impact, leaving the sweetness but deleting the power.

It all came back to Hannah now as she wound her arms around his neck and leaned into the kiss.

There was absolutely no doubt left lingering in her mind.

It had been worth the wait.

Chapter Three

It wasn't enough.

Like a single, teasing drop of water to a thirsty man, the kiss only made him want more. Crave more. Jackson struggled not to weaken any more than he already had, but it was like sinking into quicksand. The more he struggled, the deeper he sank.

Damn it, he was a man, not a boy, he wasn't supposed to be given to a boy's careless disregard of danger this way. And Hannah was that. Danger with a capital D because he'd realized that being with her for even a short amount of time made him forget all his well-ordered promises to himself, made him forget his noble ideals and effectively reduced him to a mound of needs and desires, all vying for control of him. His mind had been lost somewhere in the fray.

But somehow, though he wanted only to wrap his arms tighter around her, to deepen the kiss even more, he managed to pull himself away from the center of the vortex that had almost succeeded in sucking him in.

More shaken than he'd thought possible, he took a deep breath before he trusted himself to look into her eyes. "I'm sorry, I shouldn't have done that." Belatedly, he realized he was still holding her and abruptly dropped his hands to his sides.

Hannah felt as if something had caved in inside of her. What do you say when a man tells you he regrets kissing you?

You agree, if for no other reason than to save your pride. So she did. Pulling herself together as best she could, she raised her head with the grace of a princess facing an attacking enemy.

"No, you shouldn't have."

Why, when she was agreeing with him, did her words feel as if they were all sharpened daggers, slashing at him? Why did the look in her eyes make him feel so guilty, as if he'd just done something horrible?

Maybe he had. Jackson hurried to make what amends he could. "It's just that—"

"Just what?" she asked coolly, while her mind demanded hotly, *Talk to me, Jackson, let me know that you're not just being cruel. Give me a reason to keep my hope burning, damn it*.

Talking would only make things worse, Jackson realized. He'd never had the gift of gab. That had been Ethan's forte. Ethan had always been the one who knew what to say and when to say it. How to charm the husk right off a cob of corn. Jackson had only the truth and the truth wasn't allowed to come forth.

Picking up his bag, he did the only thing he could. He made his retreat.

"It's late, I'll—I'll see you." Jackson pulled the door shut behind him. And cursed himself for the mistake he'd just committed.

Hannah stood perfectly still, in direct contrast to the turmoil going on inside her. What had just happened here?

Was she going out of her mind? He'd just kissed her as if he'd wanted nothing more than to be with her tonight, then hurried away as if he wanted nothing more than never to see her again.

Confused, she gave up trying to make sense of any of it.

"Was that the door?"

Startled, Hannah jerked her head up and turned to see Gertie standing at the top of the stairs.

Coming down to join her, Gertie looked around and saw that there were just the two of them now. She sighed, obviously disappointed. "I was hoping he'd stay for breakfast."

There were toys to put away and a front room to straighten, neither of which were going to take care of themselves. Picking up a discarded truck, Hannah got started.

"Breakfast? You mean dinner, don't you?" Hannah asked.

Gertie followed in her wake. "I'm over half a century old, Hannah, I know what I mean. If I say breakfast, I mean breakfast." With another, even more heartfelt sigh, she shook her head. "Maybe it's too soon."

Dropping the two toys she was holding into the

large, colorful toybox, Hannah turned around and looked at Gertie suspiciously. "Too soon for what?"

The grin that took over Gertie's face was positively bawdy. "You know." She winked instead of answering specifically. "I always did think you two made a nice couple."

Hannah frowned as she threw another toy a little too hard into the toybox. "Well then, you'd be the only one."

"Oh, I don't know about that. Didn't feel the heat coming from that man's eyes when he was looking at you?" Gertie questioned.

She didn't need this right now. Hannah threw in another toy, a rabbit that bounced out as soon as he landed against the growing pile. Biting off a choice word, she picked the stuffed animal up again and this time placed it inside the toybox.

"There was no heat, Gertie." There was a warning note in her voice.

"Have it your way," Gertie sniffed. "As I recall, you always were a stubborn child."

Hannah stopped returning toys to their container and glanced toward the doorway and the stairs beyond. "Speaking of children—"

"They're asleep," Gertie assured her. "I put them both down in the nursery. They look right at home there in that big, old canopied crib."

In her redecorating plans, Hannah had sentimentally left that room just as it was. The nursery was where all seven of her great-aunt's children had slept as infants. None had reached old age. Other than being cleaned, the room had not been changed in over three-quarters of a century.

Hannah dropped the last of the toys into the toybox. "Maybe I'd better look in on them." She had a great deal of affection for Gertie, but right now, she wanted to get away from the woman's one-track conversation.

"I think you'd do better to look in on yourself," Gertie said softly just as Hannah passed her. "You're still a young girl, Hannah."

Stopping, Hannah shook her head. It had been a long time since she'd felt like a young girl. Losing her parents, her illusions and then her aunt had seen to that. "I'm thirty-one."

"That's young in my book." Gertie's chuckle sounded more like a cackle. "Heck, to an octogenarian, you're hardly more than a baby yourself."

She was being too edgy, Hannah told herself. Gertie was merely trying to be helpful. She placed her hands on the woman's shoulders. "Gertie, I know you mean well, but let it alone."

"Fine with me if you want that fine specimen of a man to be snapped up by someone else."

Gertie's remark caught Hannah's attention. Telling herself that Gertie was doing this on purpose didn't help. "Who?"

A pleased, knowing look highlighted the older woman's expression. "Jealous, are we?"

"No, I—"

Damn, she was putting her foot into it, wasn't she? But she couldn't help the curiosity that came over her. *Was* there someone in Jackson's life? Was that why she hadn't seen him since he'd returned? The town was small and gossip was the major local pastime, but she rarely had time to listen.

Gertie patted her arm. "Rest easy, there's no one else right now. I was just speaking figuratively, but mark my words, a man like Jackson won't stay on the market indefinitely."

"I'm not in the market. I've got my hands full right now." Hannah looked around the semi-straightened room. "Fuller than I bargained for."

"Well, I can stay the night, help you get your feet wet, so to speak," Gertie said.

Hannah wasn't about to impose. More than that, she wasn't going to be able to feel as if she was standing on her own two feet if she kept leaning. "I can handle it."

Gertie laughed shortly. "No woman alive can handle twins by herself the first night. Stop being so stubborn, Hannah, and let someone help you once in a while."

Hannah's affection for Gertie got the better of her. "Yes, ma'am."

"Much better." Pleased, Gertie slipped her arm around the younger woman's shoulders. "You'll take some work yet, girl, but you'll do."

By morning, the twins had given new meaning to the word *demanding*.

Hannah'd had no idea that two babies could be so difficult to manage. They didn't sleep at the same time, they slept in tandem. No sooner was Sammy asleep than Steffie was awake, her little nose dripping and her small, pitiful cries wrapping themselves around Hannah's heart.

There were hardly two winks to be rubbed together all night.

Babies or no, Hannah seriously doubted if she could have slept very much anyway. Every time there was a second in which she could close her eyes, she found herself reliving the kiss she'd experienced. She couldn't seem to remember a single kiss, a single moment of lovemaking with Ethan, but Jackson's kiss had branded her. Recalling it, her body would grow rosy, then hot and all sleep was banished indefinitely.

By morning she'd felt like death warmed over and was in no condition to face a squadron of children and their parents. Rallying, she took a cold shower and drank a hot cup of coffee. It helped. Some.

For once, the children proved to be less demanding than their parents. Word, as Hannah had suspected, had spread faster than a prairie fire. Everyone wanted to know about the babies on her doorstep. Themes and variations of the same questions were asked over and over again until her head felt like it was going to come off. Her temper was getting progressively more frayed. That, she knew, was a result of the sleepless night.

She was going to have to find a way to manage without harboring the spirit of a wounded bear, she thought, closing the front door as the last parent left that morning. It was almost noon.

Hannah sighed, closing her eyes as she leaned against the door. It took effort not to slide down to the floor against it. What she needed, she decided, was more coffee. More liquid stimulation and less of the emotional kind.

It was a moment before she sensed she wasn't alone. Hannah opened her eyes again.

Gertie, one of the twins in her arms and Angie, a

little girl of three, hanging onto the edge of her smock, stood eyeing her. Hannah straightened, squaring her shoulders.

"You look awful, girl," Gertie clucked sympathetically. "Did you get *any* sleep last night?"

"Some," Hannah lied. There was no point in discussing the whys and wherefores of her sleepless night. With luck, it was just a fluke and tonight would be better, with a return to normalcy.

Given that the babies would still be here, she sincerely doubted her own cheery prognosis.

"Yeah, right," Gertie said. "You should have woken me up. I sleep like a rock, but if you shake my shoulder, you can rouse me."

The last thing Hannah wanted was for Gertie to upbraid herself on her account. "Gertie, you're wonderful. You're already helping me out here, putting in all these hours without any pay. I just can't keep taking advantage of you like this."

The older woman's face softened into a warm smile. "It's only called taking advantage if I do it against my will. This isn't against my will, girl, I love it. Playing with these babies and caring for them is a lot more rewarding for me than sitting around, crocheting things for relatives who, when they receive them, will only wind up throwing the things away or stuffing them into boxes they'll never open."

Hannah was quickly discovering how futile it was to argue with the woman about anything. "Well, if you put it that way...."

Gertie leveled a satisfied look at her over the rim of her glasses. "I do."

The doorbell rang.

The effect of Gertie's warm assurance faded, and Hannah stiffened. She took a quick mental inventory of all the children beneath her roof. Everyone currently in her care was accounted for, including Heather Riley, whose mother had called to say the toddler would be out for the week with chicken pox.

That meant that whoever was at her door most definitely had no business being here.

Probably someone from the newspaper, Hannah thought glumly, here to do a story on the twins. She hadn't had to face that yet, but she knew it was coming just as surely as November followed October.

"I'll get that," Gertie declared.

Hannah caught her arm, stopping her. "That's all right, Gertie, I can answer my own door." A sense of acute relief flooded through her when she saw that it was Tucker on her doorstep and not some reporter from the newspaper.

Hope took anxiety's place. "Oh, Tucker, did you find the twins' mother already?"

Tucker pushed his Stetson back on his head with the edge of his thumb. "No, but I did find your mystery lady. Or rather, Penny Sue's." As he stepped out of the way, Hannah saw for the first time that Tucker wasn't alone. Recognition was instantaneous. The rest of the sheriff's words were unnecessary. "She says she's a cousin of yours, Hannah."

Caught between being stunned and overjoyed, Hannah found herself momentarily speechless. What she lacked in words she made up for in gestures. She threw her arms around the woman before her and gave her a fierce hug—as best she could. The other woman's swollen belly got in the way.

Releasing her, Hannah stepped back and drew her very pregnant cousin into the house. "Gwen, my God, Gwen, just look at you." Her eyes swept over Gwen's ripened form. "When did all this happen?"

Instinctively, Gwen placed a protective hand over her belly. "Seven months ago."

Expecting to see Gwen's husband somewhere in the near vicinity, Hannah peered out. But there was no one there.

Puzzled, she looked at Gwen. "Where's—?"

"Where he should be," Gwen said, cutting her off. "Back home."

The finality in Gwen's tone told Hannah she was treading on very sensitive terrain. Sympathy poured through her. Maybe Gwen was here waiting for some huge argument to blow over. "Is there anything I can get you?"

Gwen smiled at her cousin. "Yes, the address of a place that's renting—cheap if possible."

A small breath escaped Hannah's lips. "That final?"

Gwen nodded. "That final." She left no room for discussion.

Hannah knew what it felt like, to have a marriage die right before your eyes. To see it slip away through no fault of your own. To cover the awkwardness she knew Gwen had to be feeling right at this moment, she changed the subject. "Why were you at the back door earlier? Why not the front? And back or front, why didn't you come in?"

Gwen's smile was rueful. "I guess I was working up my courage to face you. It isn't easy coming back, letting people know things have gone wrong in your life. Besides, I wasn't at the back door. My courage petered out before I got within ten feet of your place.''

"Then it wasn't you who knocked.'' Hannah looked at Tucker. "It must have been the twins' mother,'' she guessed. Hannah slipped a comforting arm around her cousin's shoulder. "Did you happen to see anyone else around just before you lost your courage? Somebody dropped off two bundles of joy on our back steps…''

Again, Gwen shook her head. "The sheriff already asked me that when he found me in the diner. I was too preoccupied with my own problems to really see anything, I'm afraid.''

Behind her, Gertie cleared her throat rather loudly, drawing Hannah's attention to her own oversight.

"Where are my manners? Gertie, I'd like you to meet my cousin, Gwenyth Parker. Gwen, this is Gertie Anderson. And this,'' still a little flustered, Hannah turned toward Tucker, "is Sheriff Tucker Malone.''

Something akin to an amused look flittered across Tucker's face. He nodded toward Gwen. "We've already met.''

"Right, sorry.'' Hannah flashed an apologetic smile in his direction before turning toward her cousin. "I guess it's just that you caught me off balance, what with your visit and being pregnant and all.''

"The word,'' Gwen corrected kindly, "is *divorced*. I remembered what you always said about Storkville, and I thought I'd try to start a new life for myself and the baby in a place that's warm and forgiving.''

"Well then, you've certainly come to the right

place. We're warm and forgiving all right,'' Gertie assured her, taking Gwen's hand in hers and, for all intents and purposes, taking her under her wing as well.

"Thank you, Mrs. Anderson, that's very comforting to know.''

Gertie waved away the formality. "Everyone calls me Aunt Gertie and I think I might know just the place for you. There's a little house, not far from here.'' Gertie glanced at the sheriff. "You know the one I'm talking about, Tucker. The cottage on Ben Crowe's ranch. He's looking to sell it, but he might be interested in renting, you never know. It's been empty for a while.''

Familiar with the house Gertie was describing, Tucker nodded. "Right.''

After everything she'd been through, this was almost too easy. Trying to contain her excitement, Gwen looked from Gertie to Hannah. "When could I see it?''

"Well, I'm a little busy here, helping with the babies and all,'' Gertie said. "Maybe Tucker here could run you up there.''

Gwen hated imposing, but she was really eager to find a place of her own to settle into. She turned toward the sheriff hopefully. "If it wouldn't be too much trouble…''

Jumping in, Gertie curtailed any possibility of Tucker saying no. "Trouble?'' she snorted. Temporarily handing off the baby to Hannah, she took Gwen's hand. "The man doesn't know the meaning of the word trouble. Mark my words, little mother, this is the most trouble-free town ever created. Probably the most neighborly, too. Am I right, Tucker?''

"You're right, Gertie," he agreed, amused.

The picture was not as pure as Gertie was painting it, but he saw no reason to contradict her outright. Besides, it was probably futile anyway. The woman enjoyed being right. And in getting her way. Cornered, Tucker had no choice but to go along with the silent request he saw in the pregnant woman's eyes.

Stepping forward, Tucker addressed Gwen politely. "Sure. If you want to see the place, I'll take you."

"Thank you, Sheriff. All of you," she added, looking at the two women. And then she hesitated. "Would you mind if I stayed with you until all this is settled?" she asked Hannah.

"Mind?" Hannah echoed. "I insist on it."

"You're the best, Hannah," Gwen enthused.

Hannah carefully slipped Steffie back to Gertie and hugged Gwen again. "We're family. We have to stick together. You're always welcome in my home, no matter what." She knew Gwen was eager to see the house, but she had a feeling that Gwen needed reassuring more than she needed a roof over her head at the moment. Besides, if for some reason renting didn't pan out, Gwen could always stay with her indefinitely. The house was certainly big enough. "Tucker, could you put off taking Gwen to see that house for a few minutes or so? I think maybe a little tea and conversation is in order here." She looked pointedly at Gwen.

"Well, I'm not much on conversation," Tucker said, "and I'll pass on the tea, but if you have coffee—"

"Coffee it is." Hannah slipped her arm around Gwen and ushered her into the kitchen, leaving Gertie to bring up Tucker and the rear. She heard the older woman chattering away at Tucker about babies and tried not to laugh.

Half an hour later, Tucker and Gwen were at the front door, ready to leave. Just as Tucker reached for the doorknob, the doorbell rang. He noticed that Hannah, so animated only a moment ago, froze at the sound.

"Anyone been giving you trouble lately?" he wanted to know.

"No." This time, it had to be a reporter. "Just anticipating the worst."

"Woman after my own heart," Tucker said with a laugh as he pulled open the door for her.

The sound of a man's laugh registered at exactly the same moment as Jackson's excuse came tumbling from his lips. "Hannah, I thought I'd drop by during my lunch hour instead—oh."

Had he walked in on anything? Was Hannah seeing someone? That there might be a man to share her laughter, her secrets and perhaps her love, had never crossed his mind.

It did now.

Chapter Four

It took Jackson a minute to collect himself. "Sorry. I didn't mean to interrupt anything."

Tucker nodded a brusque greeting at Jackson. "You're not. We were just on our way out." His hand on the small of Gwen's back, Tucker paused in the doorway to look at Hannah. "I'll let you know if I find out anything about the twins."

Hannah nodded. "Thank you. And Gwen, after you look at the house, we need to have a proper, long visit."

"I'd like that," Gwen said, smiling.

"Me, too," Hannah assured her just before Tucker pulled the door closed behind them.

"Well, I'll just go see to the children," Gertie announced cheerfully. "Here," as an afterthought, she handed Steffie to Hannah, "you'll be needing this if you're going to take advantage of doctor-boy's kind presence here."

Aiming a triumphant smile at Jackson that left him completely mystified, Gertie took the hand of the little girl beside her and disappeared into the front room, leaving the two of them standing in the foyer, the baby between them.

Feeling awkward again, Hannah cleared her throat. "This way." This time, she led him into another room, one where she had several cribs set up for the infants she anticipated would eventually be placed in her care during the day while their parents worked. Right now, the twins were her youngest charges by a good six months.

She felt that it was her responsibility to remain in the room while he performed the quick, routine examination on Steffie, but inside, Hannah was restless, like someone who didn't know quite what to do with herself.

Jackson retired his stethoscope, placing it into his bag. "Steffie's doing about the same. Her nose is still runny, but there's no fever. How was she during the night?"

Thinking back, Hannah tried to be accurate. "She didn't cry any more than Sammy did."

That certainly sounded positive, Jackson thought. Which was more than he could say for Hannah. There was an edge to her today that hadn't been there yesterday. And she looked a little harried.

"Well, she looks pretty good, despite her runny nose." He laughed shortly, unable to refrain from commenting. "She looks better than you do."

That was something she didn't need to hear. Elbowing him out of her way, Hannah reached into the crib and began putting a fresh diaper on the baby. "You always did have a way with words."

Now he'd gone and hurt her feelings, he upbraided himself. That hadn't been his intent. Why couldn't he talk to her? He used to be able to talk to her for hours at a time.

"I didn't mean that as an insult, I was just making an observation—as a doctor."

Hannah spared him a glance over her shoulder as she powdered a freshly cleaned bottom. "Broadening your practice?"

Jackson wasn't sure if that was sarcasm or not. Once he would have known. Once, Hannah didn't have a sarcastic bone in her body, but a lot had happened since those days. He shrugged carelessly.

"It's a small town, things tend to overlap. A doctor can't afford to be rigid in his views about where his boundaries stop."

She wanted to shut the words away. They came anyway. "What about a man? Does the same rule apply?"

He studied her face for a moment, at a loss. "If this is about yesterday...I already apologized."

His answer only succeeded in getting her more agitated. She could feel her anger, so long repressed, so long banked down, beginning to flare. Slipping the romper back on the baby, she left Steffie in the crib and turned to face Jackson.

"Yes, this is about yesterday and I was wondering why you felt you had to apologize. You've done some things in your life that you should apologize for, but that really wasn't one of them."

The accusation was impossible to miss. "Oh? And what things should I have apologized for?"

She moved over to the door, closing it. She didn't want Gertie or anyone else overhearing.

"Disappearing the way you did, for one. You played Cupid, practically pushed me into Ethan's arms, and then when I married him, you didn't even stay for the reception."

"I came." He'd been best man despite his protests. He'd had no choice but to attend.

"But you didn't stay," she reminded him. He'd remained long enough to make the traditional toast. When she'd looked for him later, her mother had told her that he'd left abruptly.

"I had a plane to catch." He'd made his decision to leave town the day that Ethan had told him about the wedding. Though he had pushed them together by stepping out of the running when Ethan had confessed his feelings for Hannah to him, he knew he couldn't remain to watch the love between Ethan and Hannah blossom and bear fruit. He wasn't strong enough for that no matter how much he wished he was. A man knew his limits. "My life was taking me in other directions."

Yes, she thought, directions he purposely mapped out away from Storkville. Away from his friends and everyone who cared about him. Away from her.

But if he'd done that, why had he returned? "And now that direction has made a 180-degree about-face?"

He said the obvious, the one thing that had finally brought him back to the small town he'd promised himself he'd left behind forever. "My father died."

She knew he'd returned because of that. It had been the first thing she'd thought of when she'd heard of Jackson's death. Which was why, when Jackson had made no effort to see her after he'd come back, the sting had been almost too much for her to bear.

"That was four months ago."

"What is it you want from me, Hannah?" Jackson asked.

"An explanation. The truth. I don't know." Restless, she began to pace about the small room. "Maybe I'm just mad. Damn mad." Even as she made the admission, she could feel herself growing angrier at his abandonment. Whatever his reasons were, right now, they weren't good enough.

Her eyes blazed as she turned on him. "I could have used a friend, Jackson. When everything was falling apart around me, I could have used a friend."

He wanted to reach out and take her into his arms. He wanted to hold her and tell her he was sorry. But all he could safely do was give her his reasons, and not even much of that.

With a sigh, he shoved his hands into his pockets. "I thought I was being one by staying away."

She stared at him incredulously. Did he actually believe what he was saying?

"That's the stupidest thing I ever heard. I needed someone to talk to, to lean on. Maybe I shouldn't have, but I did—damn it," she said throwing up her hands in exasperation. "I don't even know why I'm saying this now, except that I haven't had enough sleep to keep a gnat moving, and I've got all these responsibilities in the next room." She waved in the general direction of the front room, where most of the daycare center was set up. "Not to mention these babies someone has dropped off on my doorstep and sometimes, just sometimes, I feel like hitting something or throwing something—"

He knew she wouldn't appreciate being told that she looked adorable just now, but she did. To keep her full wrath from falling on his head, Jackson did his best to suppress the smile that was struggling to get out. "Why don't you?"

Her mouth fell open. She hadn't expected him to say that.

"Because—because everything breakable in this house is an antique and precious or something, and I can't just—" Her voice trailed off into a huff as she ran out of words and steam.

"How about if I let you punch me?" As she stared at him, Jackson turned sideways, giving her unobstructed access to his upper arm. "Go ahead, take your best shot. The jacket will pad the blow," he assured her when she just stood there, staring at him. "Keep you from hurting your knuckles."

He probably thought she wouldn't. Well, she was just mad enough to do it. Doubling up her fist, she drew back and swung as hard as she could, making contact. "I don't care about my knuckles—"

The last time he'd been on the receiving end of her fist, they'd been eight. She'd got a lot stronger since then, he mused, grateful that he found time to work out. Otherwise, he had a feeling her punch might really sting, even through the jacket.

"But I do." Braced, he waited for her to swing again, and she did. Hannah swung fast and hard three times more before the energy finally went out of her swing and the fury left her eyes. He waited, but when she didn't pull her fist back again, he relaxed his arm. "Feel better?"

"Yes, thanks, I do." Hannah wiggled her fingers, looking at them. And then she looked at him and began to laugh. The tension that had been pressing down so hard on her had left. "Maybe you can add punching bag to your areas of expertise."

He rotated his shoulder. Tomorrow that was going to ache some. He figured it was worth it to see the smile on her lips and in her eyes again. "No, that's only a service I'd provide for very special friends."

She felt a little guilty now about the way she'd yelled at him. "So we still are friends?"

His eyes met hers. "Could you ever really doubt that?"

"I was beginning to," she said, talking to the man she'd once known, not the stranger who'd returned to town four months ago. "You did drop out of our lives rather abruptly."

He thought of what he could safely tell her without revealing her the complete truth. "I didn't want to intrude."

She just didn't understand what could have been going through his mind, or how he could ever think this way. "How could you have ever intruded? The three of us grew up together. Our lives were entwined for all time." Her voice softened as she remembered. "There was a time I could finish your sentences and you could finish mine."

He remembered that. Remembered, too, how feeling that way had made him believe, for just a little while, that maybe for him things could be different.

But he was faced with evidence of the contrary almost every time he turned around. The apple never fell far from the tree, and the tree he had come from had roots that were rotten.

"Maybe I was afraid that Ethan would be jealous of that. He was my best friend, I didn't want to give him any cause for jealousy. Besides, things change when you get married." He thought of his own parents, of how his mother had told him how attentive his father had been to her until they had gotten married. And of all the women who had come along in the wake of those vows.

"Yes," she agreed quietly, "they do." And Ethan had changed after their vows had been exchanged. Not at first. In those early months, with the excitement of the adventure they faced still fresh, he'd been every bit the loving husband. Or so he had seemed.

But slowly, the freshness had faded and, with it, Ethan's attentions.

This wasn't the time to dwell on that. She didn't want Jackson reading things in her expression, didn't want to mar the image he carried in his mind of his best friend.

"So," she asked brightly, "do I have anything to be concerned about with Steffie?"

"Not really. I'd just watch her. Continue doing what you were doing. I'd say keep her away from her brother until her sniffles are gone, but it's probably too late for that."

She couldn't resist picking Steffie up and holding her for a moment. There was something so soft, so endearing about the small bundle. "You mean because they came in together?"

He nodded. She looked good like that, he thought. Natural. Someone like Hannah should have a brood of kids all around her. Her own kids. He felt a pang at the thought.

"The time they're really contagious is during the incubation time, which means that if he's going to come down with anything, he's already caught it."

Hannah thought of Sammy. There'd been no indication that he was congested or even harboring anything. "He seemed fine during the night and this morning."

"Could be he gave it to her, or maybe her cold will bypass him. Just because they share space doesn't necessarily mean they'll share the germs." He couldn't help grinning at the bemused expression on her face. She seemed overwhelmed, but if he knew Hannah, she'd manage. She always did. "That's what keeps it interesting," he confided. "I wouldn't worry about it. They both seem like very healthy babies."

She couldn't help looking down at the face of the baby against her breast. "Makes you wonder why someone would just toss them away like that, doesn't it?"

If they had been hers, there was no way she would have ever allowed herself to be separated from them, let alone willingly leave them. What kind of a mother did something like that?

"They didn't toss them away," he pointed out. "They gave them to you to care for." He followed her out into the hall.

He made it sound almost like a selfless action, but she had her doubts about that.

"I have a feeling that whoever left them had no

idea who they were leaving them with. They were just hoping someone would feel sorry for the twins and take are of them.''

"A stranger?'' he guessed. Hannah nodded. Jackson rolled the thought around in his mind, deciding it was more than possible. "Well, Storkville does have a reputation.''

"Penny Sue,'' she called. "Could you take Steffie for me? It's time for her lunch. Ask Gertie to help you with Sammy.''

Appearing, Penny Sue tossed her hair over her shoulders proudly. "I can take care of them, it's just a little feeding.''

"Famous last words,'' Gertie declared, eyeing the young girl as she came up next to her. "I'll handle things here,'' Gertie assured Hannah. "You just take care of the good doctor here.'' She all but shooed her out of the room. "C'mon, children,'' she declared to the other nine children, "we're going to play a game called Watch Gertie Feed the Babies.''

"She's a good woman,'' Hannah said. "I don't know what I would do without her. But I really wish Gertie had come up with a better name when she started her little legend about Storkville. Makes us sound like something out of a storybook.''

The notion made Jackson smile. "Maybe sometimes you are.''

"Oh? What kind of a storybook?'' She realized that she was flirting with him—and that it felt good. "Something to do with princesses and dragons?''

He pretended to let that sink in. "Yes, I could see you as a princess.'' And if truth be told, he already had. More than once. An unattainable princess he could never hope to possess.

She laughed softly. It was good to talk like this, teasingly, the way they had in the old days.

"Thanks, I really needed that." And then a hint of mischief curved her mouth. "You realize that if you'd said you could see me as the dragon, I would have had to kill you."

When she looked at him like that, with laughter shimmering in her eyes, all he could think of was kissing her again and somehow sharing in that laughter, having it filter into his own soul. "No danger there. You're not the one I see as a dragon in this story."

He sounded so serious just then, it was almost as if they hadn't regained old ground at all. "Then who?"

He waved away her question and his own slip of the tongue. "Doesn't matter, the dragon's gone." It was just his legacy that lived on, Jackson added silently.

He was being awfully mysterious, Hannah thought, but there was something in Jackson's eyes that kept her from asking who he was talking about. She told herself that it was enough that they had dropped some of their armor, that she had managed to clear the air and that they were slowly getting back on the footing they'd once held.

She glanced back into the front room. Gertie and Penny Sue seemed to have things under control. Silently, she blessed them, then looked at Jackson.

"You said you were on your lunch hour. Can I fix you something to eat?"

He glanced at his watch. It was getting ... had a two o'clock appointment coming in. ... better be getting back. I'm cutting it short as ...

"Business that good?"

"This is the town for babies," he reminded her.

He was rushing away from her. Yesterday, she would have let him leave. But she'd glimpsed the way things had once been between them and it gave her hope that they could be that way again. So she stalled a little.

"Sure I can't tempt you with anything?"

That was just the problem, she could and he wasn't sure just how up he was to resisting that temptation, no matter how much he knew that he should. "No, that's okay."

He'd given up his lunch hour to look in on Steffie. The least she could do was feed him, Hannah thought. "How about a sandwich to go?" She saw him wavering. Jackson probably hadn't eaten anything all day. She remembered how he used to forget to eat when he got involved in something. "I make a mean peanut butter and jelly sandwich."

He laughed. "I haven't had one of those since—" he looked at her, bits and pieces of memories coming back to him "—we used to play house together."

"It wasn't house," she corrected him primly, though her eyes were dancing. "It was club." She slipped her arm through his, subtly directing him toward the kitchen. "You and Ethan were very specific about that. You didn't want any of your friends seeing you doing anything the least bit unmanly. I guess manhood was a big deal for a ten-year-old."

That took him back. If he closed his eyes, he could

still see their clubhouse. They'd built it themselves, the three of them, out of discarded wood left over from a guest house Ethan's father had built on the property. They'd had the devil's own time, dragging the planks up into the tree. In the end, it had been Hannah who had managed better than they. She'd gloried in showing them up, a scrawny girl pitted against two boys.

The memory pleased him. "You climbed better than any boy I ever knew."

Something lit up inside Hannah. She liked seeing him smile. "The treehouse is still up, you know."

He didn't know. He'd expected it, like all things from childhood, to have been taken down long ago. "You're kidding."

Hannah shook her head. "Nope." The clubhouse had been constructed on Ethan's parents' property. She and Ethan had lived at the house after his parents moved to Denver. "Ethan wanted to have the tree removed. He said it was in the way." She'd been upset when she discovered him talking to a gardening service, pricing the cost of the removal. She felt as if the last bastion of her childhood was under attack. "Some grand plans for a huge pool, but I argued for the treehouse."

"And you won." As he recalled, she always could argue better than either one of them.

Hannah slipped her arm from his. She shrugged carelessly, not wanting to get into that. "It never really got resolved. Ethan was killed in that car accident that same weekend."

"I'm sorry I wasn't here." He'd said that already, yesterday, but noble reasons or not, he should have come, Jackson thought. He should have attended the services. But he was afraid of what the sight of Hannah weeping at Ethan's grave would do to him. And what it might make him do, or say to her.

"I could have used you," she told him truthfully. "But there really wasn't anything you could have done. I handled the arrangements and made the best of it." It almost seemed as if all that had happened in another lifetime, to another woman. "Life goes on, right?"

"Yeah, it's been known to."

"Anyway, let me fix you that sandwich. By the way, what do house calls go for these days? I forgot to ask yesterday." She opened the cupboard and took out a jar of raspberry jam and a jar of peanut butter. "I remember my grandmother said she used to pay the doctor three dollars when he stopped by the house, but that was before house calls went out of style." A loaf of bread plucked out of the refrigerator joined the jars on the counter.

He watched her hands as she worked. It was safer than looking at her eyes. "One peanut butter sandwich should take care of it—as long as you put in extra peanut butter."

Laughing, she dipped the knife back into the jar. "Extra peanut butter it is."

Tucker returned with Gwen shortly after Jackson left. Gwen had tentatively rented the house, but it wouldn't be ready to move in to for a couple of weeks and it was agreed that she would stay with Hannah until then. Since Hannah refused any form of payment, Gwen insisted on helping her at the daycare center. Counting Rebecca Fielding, the new ob/gyn who sporadically dropped by the center to volunteer her services, Hannah had almost more volunteers than she knew what to do with. It was a nice feeling.

Tucker surprised her by returning a third time just after parents began arriving to pick up their children. Hannah left Gertie to the task of ushering off the children, knowing there was nothing the woman enjoyed better than visiting with their parents, while she took Tucker into the small parlor.

"Just thought you'd want to know that your initial instincts that the twins' mother might be from out of town were right on the money," he told her, running the rim of his Stetson through his hands. "I asked around and Penny Sue's father recalls seeing a woman driving a beat-up old pickup on the outskirts of town, heading west. Being Penny Sue's father, he couldn't help jotting down the license plate. But he only got part of it down. Doesn't correspond to any vehicle from around here."

"Was it an out-of-state license?" If it was, she thought, that made the search that much more difficult.

"No, as a matter of fact, the license was issued in Nebraska. I'm going to put in a call to the DMV in Omaha. Got a friend working there. See if he can come up with anything."

"On just a partial plate? They can do that?"

"You'd be surprised what they can do," he'd said, moving toward the foyer. "It'll take time, but right now, that's the only thing we've got to go on. We're not making much headway with the rattle." He'd almost forgotten. Reaching into his jacket, he took out a legal envelope from his pocket. "In the meantime, I got the court order from the judge, making this official." He handed the envelope to her. "The twins are now legally in your custody until we can get this all resolved."

Accepting the envelope, she held it for a moment without opening it. "I hope nobody's going to regret this."

At the front door, Tucker covered the knob with his hand. "Give yourself a little credit, Hannah. The rest of us have all got faith in you."

"Well, I always wanted to be a mother, I guess this'll show me if I'm cut out for the job."

"No doubt in my mind," he told her, leaving.

Yes, she thought, but there was certainly doubt in hers.

Chapter Five

Hannah wasn't sure exactly what drew her to it, only that she had a sudden, irresistible urge to visit the old tree house that stood on her late husband's property. Standing in the moonlight at the foot of the old oak, looking up at the square structure nestled in its branches, a wave of sentimentality washed over Hannah so completely, it was difficult for her to draw a deep breath.

She had no idea why she felt tears stinging her eyes. It was silly. Maybe she was developing allergies. Or getting Steffie's cold. Sniffing, she blinked the tears back.

Maybe it was seeing Jackson again that had drawn her here, or maybe it was just an overwhelming urge to revisit a time when there were no responsibilities, no hurt feelings and life had held the promise of an endless, joyful surprise. Whatever it was, she just couldn't help herself. She had had to come back to see it again.

So, after the daycare center was officially closed for the day and Penny Sue had left, she'd asked Gertie if she'd mind staying and watching the twins for about half an hour. Just long enough for her to spend a few minutes here. She didn't want to leave Gwenyth alone to cope with everything her first evening.

Gertie had taken Hannah's sweater off the coat rack, shoved it into her hands and all but pushed her out the door. She had looked well pleased that Hannah was getting out of the house and told her to take her time.

She, Ethan and Jackson had built their beloved tree house in the oak tree that was located in the middle of the backyard. It was sufficiently far away from the house to allow the three young building partners to pretend they were off on their own, yet close enough for their parents to be able to look out and make sure that everything was all right.

At least Ethan's parents had looked, as had her own from the house next door. Jackson's parents, as she recalled, had never come looking for him or wondered where he was.

Thinking about it now, she remembered that the Caldwells had never given any indication that Jackson had any rules restricting him. She and Ethan had curfews, but not Jackson. Jackson could stay out as long as he liked, stay away as long as he wanted. No one seemed to care.

She supposed that was why he'd seemed so dark and attractive to her. He was the very image of the young, brooding rebel. A rebel with kind eyes.

Ethan had envied Jackson his freedom, but she hadn't. Not really. In her heart, though she'd never admitted it, she'd felt sorry for Jackson. She felt that there was something lacking in a life where you didn't have your parents to fall back on. A life where you couldn't be certain that they would be there to catch you if you fell and hold you if you hurt. She'd never gotten anything but a sense of there being distance between Jackson and his parents and it made her sad for him.

But Jackson had acted as if it didn't bother him at all, as if the freedom Ethan envied him was the greatest thing in the world.

Some had considered him wild in those days. She'd just thought of him as untamed and thrilling to be with.

Certainly nobody who knew Jackson Caldwell Jr. had ever expected him to grow up to become a doctor, let alone a pediatrician. Pediatricians had to have an affinity for children, and no one had thought that Jackson could have feelings like that.

Mostly, she supposed, the town had figured he'd grow up to be a spoiled rich kid coming to no good, the way so many others had before him.

A soft smile curved her mouth. She'd known better, even then. She'd known that the person who existed just beneath the carefully crafted facade was someone entirely different. It was that person she'd spent hours talking to. That person who she felt had become her very best friend. And he had been—then. Oh, she'd told people that it was Ethan because of course you were supposed to say the man were going to marry was your best friend, but even when they had shared the initial intimacy of marriage, Ethan had never been as close to her soul as Jackson had been.

Which was why when Jackson had left town so abruptly, she'd felt like a piece of her had been permanently ripped away. An irretrievable piece she was never going to be able to recover or replace.

Her loss had only intensified when Ethan began coming home late, began making up excuses for missing occasions and forgetting about important dates—like their second anniversary. They'd made reservations for dinner at the restaurant where he had proposed to her. She'd dined alone. He'd been incredibly repentant immediately thereafter, inundating her with flowers and a beautiful gold pin she never wore. The gifts meant nothing because the sentiment wasn't real. The Ethan she'd thought she loved wasn't real. And the real Ethan didn't change.

After a while, she'd felt completely adrift, betrayed by the very ideals she'd clung to so tightly while she'd been growing up.

But she hadn't come here to think about lost ideals, she'd come to try, for a moment, to recapture a happier time. A time when she had loved everything and everyone and been so full of hope.

She wanted that feeling back, if only for a little while.

Testing the wooden slats she vividly remembered hammering into the tree with Ethan and Jackson, Hannah slowly climbed up. The tree house seemed smaller, but the climb felt steeper. One of the slats creaked ominously, but it held, as did the others.

Carefully, she made her way inside what was little more than a wooden box with a doorway and two windows carved out. She couldn't help the smile that came to her lips. If anyone had happened by, they'd have probably thought she'd lost her mind.

But she was hungry for a tiny piece of the past.

Maybe, like everything else, revisiting this faraway portion of her life would prove disappointing. Everyone said you couldn't go home again. She wondered if that meant to tree houses as well.

There was debris on the wooden floor, swept inside by more than seventeen years of storms that had come and gone since the last time she had been here. As she found a space for herself on the floor, a spider quickly scurried out of the way.

"Don't worry," she murmured to it, "I'm not moving in. Just visiting."

Very slowly, she looked around. It was so much smaller than she remembered. But then, the last time they had all sat here, they'd been fourteen, on the cusp of entering high school and a whole different world had been beckoning to them. The tree house had seemed hopelessly childish then. A remnant of their past. Right now, it seemed only incredibly sweet, if somewhat cramped.

Ethan had wanted to give it a Viking burial back then, she recalled. One last hurrah before they entered high school. It had been Jackson who'd pointed out the danger in that flashy act. She'd always wondered if he'd opposed Ethan because he'd actually had a practical side to him, or because he's seen how upset she'd been at the thought of destroying something that had been such a large part of their lives. To her, the tree house had symbolized a bond that had been forged between the three of them.

She supposed she'd never know what Jackson's reasons were for stopping Ethan. Either way, Ethan had reluctantly agreed, though lamenting that it would have made a wondrous sight, visible to the whole town—before the fire department could come to put it out. That day, Ethan had been the reckless one while Jackson had been the voice of practicality. Hannah should have picked up on that.

The boards beneath her creaked unexpectedly even though she hadn't shifted. She didn't weigh all that much more than she had at fourteen, but time and weather had taken their toll on the tree house and she wondered if she was taking unnecessary chances, being here. What if the planks broke and she fell? She certainly couldn't afford to get hurt now.

Daycare center owner foolishly climbed into her old tree house and fell through the rotting floor. Stay tuned to your local news. Film at eleven.

Biting back a grin, she decided to stay a few more minutes before going back to her house. She couldn't remain here for long, anyway. Gertie had to go home. It wouldn't be fair to make her stay another night, no matter how much she protested that she enjoyed helping out with the twins.

The twins were her responsibility, not Gertie's or Gwenyth's.

Moonlight winked in through the window that faced the back of the yard. Looking through it now, if she tried very hard, she could even catch a glimpse of Jackson's house. Located further up on the winding hill, the Caldwell estate looked down on the rest of them like a feudal lord looking down on the surrounding peasants who made up his fiefdom. When she'd been a lot younger, she'd secretly thought of Jackson as a prince, a dark, brooding prince who'd someday come galloping into her chambers and rescue her. From what, she wasn't sure. The very act would have been sufficient to win her tender heart.

Funny how he'd commented about her being a princess earlier today. Maybe, she mused, they were still in tune to one another a little bit after all.

Hannah sighed. She'd indulged herself long enough. It was time to go back before Gertie thought she'd abandoned her.

Getting up on her knees, she made her way to the opening, taking care not to move too fast and tempt fate in the form of a loose board.

Then she gasped. Rocking back on her heels, she stared at the person blocking her way out of the tree house.

Jackson.

Automatically she placed a hand over the heart that was even now racing madly. "What are you doing here?"

He was as stunned to see her as she was to see him. Finding Hannah here had been the furthest thing from his mind. He'd heard she'd rented out the house where she and Ethan had lived, but that the people were away on an end-of-summer vacation. Hannah was supposed to be at her own home now, not here.

Pleasure spilled out through him and he grinned at her question. "The peanut butter sandwich you gave me for lunch made me nostalgic. Can I come in? I forgot the password."

"Passwords," she corrected, backing up so he could make his way inside. "Passwords. One for all,

all for one." That had been her idea, conceived right after she'd read *The Three Musketeers*. It had seemed so very romantic and dashing to her, though she hadn't said as much. She didn't want Ethan and Jackson to laugh at her. Especially not Jackson.

"Right." It came back to him. The floor felt rough and dirty beneath his hands as he made his way in. "I should have remembered that."

Why should he? He hadn't remembered to live the credo, she thought. The rebuke was hot on her tongue, but she let it go. What was the point?

Their faces inches away from one another, he tried to put temptation out of his mind. Instead, he watched her catch her lower lip in her teeth as Hannah look around at the tree house uncertainly. "I'm not sure this can support both of us."

For once, it looked as if he had more faith than she did, Jackson thought. "Sure it can. Don't you remember how handy we were? We built this tree house to last forever."

"We built it to last forever for three skinny kids," she reminded him.

Still on all fours, he let his eyes sweep over her quickly, trying his best to seem detached and professional. If he pulled that off, he was probably a better actor than he gave himself credit for, he thought.

"Well, by the looks of you, you haven't gained very much in all that time and I don't think I weigh more than Ethan and I did put together back then. It'll hold up for at least a quick visit."

Jackson sat down in the center, crossing his legs before him. Listening for any telltale groans, Hannah followed suit, facing him. She told herself she was having trouble breathing because of the dust in the air, not because she was sitting here in the moonlight with a man she had loved for more than half her life.

Looking around, Jackson shook his head, marveling. "What did we do in here for all those hours?"

"Lots of things," she told him, pretending to take umbrage that he could have so easily forgotten something so precious. "We talked, read comics, made plans. Thought about the future. Remember how there were times when we thought it would never come? That we were going to stay ten years old forever?"

"Yeah, but by the time we hit fourteen, the future was just right outside, reaching out to us and we couldn't wait to get to it."

He remembered making plans even back then to leave home and the shame that never seemed to be that far away from him. That was when he'd still believed he could outrun his heritage, that it was possible to distance himself from what haunted him.

She shrugged. She had never been as eager as either Ethan or Jackson had been to forge ahead. Maybe it was because she'd never wanted things to change. "I don't know. Right now, the past looks better."

He thought she was referring to Ethan's sudden death. "I can understand that." Jackson had no idea how to convey his sympathy to her. The news of Ethan's accident had hit him very hard as well. "I know it had to hurt a great deal, losing Ethan like that."

Hannah pressed her lips together. What was the sense of telling him that the pain of losing Ethan had come long before Tucker had walked into her house that muggy summer afternoon, and told her Ethan had died instantly in a head-on collision with a truck whose driver had lost control of the wheel. Because he was kind, Tucker had tried to keep from her the fact that there was someone else in the car with Ethan. Another woman. The last in a long line. But she'd found out soon enough.

It wasn't anything she hadn't come to expect.

But Jackson obviously wasn't aware of any of this, or of Ethan's insatiable quest for women. What was the point in shattering any illusions Jackson might still have about his former best friend? "Yeah," was all she said.

There were spaces now between the boards they had nailed together so diligently, spaces that allowed the wind to come whistling through. "Wind's picking up," Jackson noted. "Maybe we'd better take this trip down memory lane somewhere where it's warmer. Can't have you getting sick."

For her part, she wouldn't have minded staying here a little longer and absorbing the memories. But he was right, they should be getting back.

She smiled. "If I do, I know a great doctor."

About to get up, he stopped. She was looking at him strangely. "What?"

"Nothing." But his look urged her on. "Okay, I have to admit it. I'm still having a little trouble picturing Storkville's bad boy being a pediatrician."

He grinned. At times, it surprised him, too. But it was all part of his desire to be as different a man from his father as he could. "Well, I did go to medical school. That should have given you some kind of clue I was serious about being a doctor."

She offered no apologies. "I thought maybe you

were doing it because it was easier going to school than trying to be respectable.''

He supposed that was to be expected. Because his father was the kind of womanizer he was, because Jackson himself had gone out of his way to break rules and stir up trouble, he could see why his final career choice would be such a surprise for not only her but for the rest of the town.

''I wasn't that bad. A few harmless pranks, my father always made restitution.'' And exacted payment out of his hide for it in private twice over, Jackson remembered. But that wasn't anything he'd ever shared with anyone, not even Hannah.

Thinking back now, as he looked at her, he remembered that it was Hannah more than Ethan who had shared the thoughts he had been willing to impart. Hannah who had kept his counsel and his secrets. Always Hannah.

And Hannah had married Ethan. With not only his blessings, but his urgings, he reminded himself.

''It wasn't the pranks that made you the town's bad boy, Jackson.''

''Oh, then what?'' he asked.

Hannah closed her eyes for a second, going back in time. When she opened them again, she realized that the journey hadn't been necessary. This, at least, hadn't really changed. It still made her heart race just to look at him.

''There was something in your eyes, something about you. That air of danger.'' And it was still there, she thought. Just beneath the surface. That edgy danger that made a woman's skin tingle just to be near it.

Jackson laughed, shaking his head. "You're romanticizing."

The romantic in her had faded away almost three years ago. "I'm remembering," she corrected. And then she smiled at him again. "That's what I always liked about you, you never knew the effect you had on the girls around you. Or the women. You never had a swelled head."

Unlike Ethan, she added silently. Ethan had known exactly the kind of power he had over women. And had known just how to use it. Her mistake, now that she looked back, was that she'd never realized it.

He waved away the words. She was letting their friendship color her judgment. Yes, there had been girls, lots of them. And though he had enjoyed them, he had known exactly what they were after at the time.

"They were attracted to the Caldwell name. And the Caldwell money." He realized that had to sound bitter to her and he tempered his voice. "You and Ethan were probably my only real friends."

Closest, maybe, she allowed. Certainly no one had cared about him more than she had. And Ethan had always stuck up for Jackson, that much she could say about him. But she laughed at the poor-little-rich-boy image that came to mind.

"Nobody would have ever guessed, seeing you. You could have had your pick of girls. They were always around." And she knew he had slept with some of them. Knowing that had kept her awake nights, hurting. Wishing he would notice her that way. But he never did. "Why didn't you ever marry anyone?"

He hadn't expected that question coming from her. He shrugged carelessly.

"Because I never found anyone genuine enough." Jackson looked at her. *And because I was already in love with you.* What would she say if he said that to her? Would she think he was teasing her? Or would she draw away, upset that her husband's best friend had had feelings for her? "I guess some men are just confirmed bachelors."

"And some men are five feet three, but you're neither."

She said it with such conviction. Had he done something to give himself away, to make her suspect the depth of the feelings he'd always had for her? He'd kissed her, but she had to have had a great many other men do that.

"What makes you think so?"

"I know you too well. Confirmed bachelors fall into two camps," she said. "The ones in the first camp are womanizers who just want to have their fun and move on. The ones in the second camp are woman haters and want to have nothing to do with the fairer sex." She looked at him pointedly. "Neither description fits you."

There was something about her, sitting here with the moon highlighting her, that twisted his gut with longing for things that could have been, had he been anyone but who he was. "You're absolutely sure of that?"

"Absolutely," she whispered. He looked as if he was going to kiss her. *Oh please, let him kiss me.*

But instead, he drew back. "You always could argue for hours."

She tried not to sound as disappointed as she felt. "Everyone needs a hobby."

It was time to go, before he gave in to the temptations ravaging him right now and took her, here and now, in the place where their innocence had been maintained so well.

"Mine's making sure people don't get sick. Sitting in tree houses when the temperature's dropping isn't part of that." He nodded toward the doorway. "Want to go first, or should I lead the way?"

She swallowed, giving up the moment, telling herself she'd only been imagining things anyway. "You go first, I'll follow."

As it turned out, it proved to be a good plan, because otherwise, she might have broken her ankle or something equally as vital. Just as Hannah was on the third to the last board on the tree, it finally gave way, cracking beneath her foot. A tiny gasp escaped her lips as she felt herself falling.

The next moment, she felt Jackson's arms closing around her, pulling her to him. Saving her.

Chapter Six

The air left her lungs as if it had been sucked out by some huge, old fashioned blacksmith bellows. It was the proximity of the man, not the fall itself that had done it.

Grasping his arms to steady herself, Hannah could have sworn she felt Jackson's heart beating just above hers. And just as quickly.

"As the closest doctor in the immediate vicinity, I prescribe that you not go climbing into tree houses anymore." A hint of a smile moved across his lips. "Or at least not until they can be retro-fitted for safety," Jackson said, loosening his arms and holding her away from him.

She didn't want to back away just yet. She knew she should, but she just couldn't seem to back away. Cocking her head, she looked up at him, memorizing every plane, every contour of his face. As if it wasn't already branded in her mind and in her heart. "Have anyone in mind to do the retro-fitting?"

He willed his hands to release her, and found only disobedience. "I'm still pretty handy with a hammer and nails."

A vision of Jackson, his shirt off and sweat glistening on his skin, came to her. It took a second for her to find her tongue. "Do you come cheap? I can't afford to pay much."

As if he could ever take money from her, even if he had needed it. He'd heard that Ethan had left her with a mountain of debts to pay off. Her great-aunt had left the house, and a way out for her, just in time.

"We can work something out."

Work something out. God, how desperately she wanted to work something out. "Promise?"

The smile softened the features of his face, making him seem almost boyish instead of a man in his third decade of life. "No promises, remember? If you don't make promises, then you can't accidentally break them."

But you can, she thought. You can make promises with your eyes. The way he had with her. But whether he said them aloud or not, he had always been there for her. Until her wedding day.

Hannah struggled against a wave of bittersweet feelings. She lost.

Before she could dig in again, she found herself being swept away. Not being able to stem the tide, she went with her feelings, with her instincts.

With her needs.

Rising up on her toes so that her mouth was level with his, she pressed her lips to Jackson's. She couldn't have said what possessed her to do it, to turn soft banter into softer intimacy, except that every fiber of her being had wanted it. Begged for it.

She needed to kiss him, to have his lips against hers again. She needed to feel that wild, intoxicated emotion surging through her, taking her prisoner as it went on a wild and all-too-fleeting ride.

Jackson had been struggling with himself, struggling not to kiss her. Struggling to do the right thing. Suddenly, the decision was taken out of his hands.

All his noble intentions turned to ashes. With the taste of her mouth against his, her sweetness robbed him of his ability to think, leaving him only to react. He lost his train of thought and took advantage of the moment and the opportunity.

Tightening his arms around her slender form again, he felt her body pressed against his as he deepened the kiss and fell head long into it.

All his life, things had come easily to him—except the one thing he'd wanted. Hannah. He wanted to discover all her secrets, worshipping every inch of her body here under the dusky blanket of twilight.

And then what? his mind silently demanded. Wait for the other shoe to drop? Wait until something made him move on, made him leave her? Made him hurt Hannah the way his father had hurt his mother? It was only a matter of time.

He was too much his father's son to discount the reality of that. Whenever he looked into the mirror, he saw his father's eyes looking back at him. His father's face. While he'd been growing up, everyone had always been quick to point out how much he resembled his father, how many similarities there were between them, whether in athletic prowess or in the way that women would flock to them both.

Jackson didn't want to be his father. He couldn't change his looks or his abilities, but he could do something about the detractions. He could be selfless and rein in his own desires to keep the inevitable from transpiring.

That meant not allowing his feelings to get in the way of what he knew was the right thing to do.

But it was so damn hard when he was standing in the moonlight like this, holding Hannah in his arms. Wanting her. When he could feel her, warm and pliant and willing, against him. When he could taste her hunger and it matched his own.

Damn him, he thought, he was taking advantage of her vulnerability. What kind of a man was he?

Hannah could feel him withdrawing, could pinpoint the instant Jackson's thoughts intruded into what had been, only a second before, a glorious physical moment.

He left her. Left her as surely as if he'd taken the actual steps away from her.

Shaken, she drew back. A woman had her pride, even if there wasn't much of it left.

She looked down, avoiding his eyes. "Sorry, I guess my lips must have tripped, too."

Passing his palm along her cheek, he raised her head until she was forced to meet his gaze. "Don't ever be sorry, Hannah. You have nothing to be sorry for. It's me who should be apologizing to you."

Did he have any idea how much that stung? It took effort to keep her voice steady, to keep her emotion from flowing into it. "For what?"

"For kissing you. Before and now." He regretted it, sorely, regretted sampling what he shouldn't, what he couldn't have.

Why? her mind screamed. Why did it seem so wrong to him to have feelings for her? She interpreted it the only way she knew how.

"Is this because of some loyalty you feel you owe Ethan?" she asked. When Jackson made no response, she took it for agreement. Anger at the unfairness of the burden of the secret she had to bear broke through. "Maybe if you'd stayed around to get to know Ethan, you wouldn't feel so badly about what just happened."

"I did know Ethan. What are you saying?"

"Nothing." What was the sense of dragging up the things that went on between a husband and wife? Of the disillusion that was the hallmark of her marriage? Maybe if he knew, Jackson would even put the blame on her for what had happened. And maybe part of it *was* her fault. How many nights had she lain awake, thinking that if only she'd be more of a woman she could hold on to her man? There were far too many to count.

She shook her head, regretting the slip. "I'm tired, Jackson." She tried to get past him but he caught her arm.

His eyes searched her face, looking for a clue, for something more to go on. But her expression was impassive, her eyes flat. "Is there something I should know, Hannah?" he pressed.

Her temper flared again. "Yeah, in your heart. Right there," she poked at his chest with her finger, "that's where you should know." And then she caught herself. What was the matter with her? Mustering a contrite smile, she shook her head again. "Never mind. Forget what I just said. It's just exhaustion talking. I'm going home now. I suggest you do the same." Hannah walked by him, her perfume lingering in the air in her wake. "Good night, Jackson. It was nice reminiscing with you."

He stood looking at her go, knowing that if he went after her, one of them would regret it. He couldn't afford for it to be her.

She'd been waiting for him. Knowing she shouldn't, she still did.

Throughout the next morning, no matter what Hannah was doing, whether it was taking care of the twins, or playing with the children, or talking to the parents who came to drop them off, Hannah kept listening for the doorbell to ring just one more time. Although she knew she shouldn't, she was waiting for Jackson. Waiting to hear his familiar footfall on her front step.

All the while she was calling herself an idiot. By noon she had graduated to a hopeless idiot.

But when Jackson finally did arrive, all her self-deprecating upbraidings went out the window the second she opened the door. They blew away when she saw the flowers in his hand. Not flowers neatly swaddled in a long box and lying on a bed of green tissue paper, but flowers from the bushes that surrounded his house. He'd picked red roses for her. Her very favorite.

It took a second to clear away the lump in her

throat. She raised her eyes to his, hoping she wouldn't do something stupid, like cry.

"You remembered."

Jackson walked into the foyer and she closed the door behind him. "Hard not to remember, you used to steal them all the time when you were younger," he said.

Hannah sniffed. He would remember that. "I didn't steal them."

His eyes crinkled slightly. "What do you call cutting them off and taking them away?"

"Borrowing." She grinned, taking the bouquet into her hands. "I just never got around to returning them."

The look of pure pleasure on her face was worth more than the most priceless jewels. "Am I forgiven?"

"You're forgiven." She laughed, turning the bouquet around. The next moment she winced. "Ow."

"What?" His eyes immediately lowered to her hands. "I shaved off all the thorns." He'd taken extra care, just as he'd seen the gardener do for his mother when he'd been a boy.

"Well, I think you missed one." She held up her finger as proof. A single drop of blood oozed from the fresh wound. "No harm done."

She was about to pop the finger into her mouth, the way she might have with any minor cut, when he took her hand in his. Her heart flipped over as she watched him do exactly what she'd intended, slipping the wounded finger between his own lips.

Her eyes held his as a wide sliver of excitement shimmied all through her.

"Very doctor-like of you," she teased. Teased because if she didn't, she was going to throw herself into his arms again and embarrass both of them.

His smile went right to her inner core, setting it on fire. "Some time-honored traditions a doctor knows not to tamper with. Maybe I'd better go take a look to see how Steffie and Sammy are doing," he suggested.

Struggling with the hot, pink blush that was fighting to overtake all of her, Hannah dropped her hand to her side. "Maybe."

"You know," Gertie murmured to Hannah, taking the topic out of the blue as she was wont to do whenever the whim moved her, "for a man with a thriving practice and hardly much time to breathe, Jackson Caldwell certainly does seem to come around here often enough." She took a large tray of hot oatmeal chocolate chip cookies out of the oven and slid it onto the stove top.

It'd been more than a week since the babies had appeared on Hannah's doorstep. More than a week with no more leads than had initially been discovered. And Jackson had made it a point to stop by each day, either during his lunch break or after office hours to look in on the twins, monitoring their progress.

Though she tried not to, telling herself she was just setting herself up for a fall, Hannah looked forward to the visits. Waited for them.

But she tried to look nonchalant as she defended Jackson's actions. "He comes here as a favor to me, to check the babies out."

"Uh-huh." Wiping her hands on her apron, Gertie

gave her a knowing look. "That's not all he's checking out."

With Penny Sue and Gwenyth in the front room with the children, Hannah began to prepare a plate of cookies to take to them for their afternoon snack. "Maybe he's afraid they might be harboring something or coming down with something."

Gertie dismissed the excuse with a short laugh. "Ask me, it's the good doctor who's finally come down with something—and it's high time, too." Hannah stopped piling cookies and gave Gertie a warning look. "Don't give me that look, Hannah Dawson. I've got eyes."

The last thing she wanted was Gertie spreading rumors. Friendly, outgoing and everyone's grandmother, the woman was on a first-name basis with the entire town. "Well, they obviously need to be rechecked, and it's Hannah Brady, not Hannah Dawson, remember?"

"That was just a temporary aberration." Taking out the second tray and resting it beside the first, Gertie took a deep breath, growing serious. "You married the wrong man, Hannah."

She knew that now, maybe knew that then, but being told so frayed her temper. "I married the man who asked me, Gertie. The man who said he loved me and wanted to make me his wife." And Jackson hadn't. Ever.

Gertie saw the distress in Hannah's eyes. "Sorry. Didn't mean to get you upset." Momentarily contrite, Gertie looked away. "Sometimes I just run off at the mouth when I shouldn't."

Nothing like a retraction to stir up her guilt, Hannah thought. She laid a hand on Gertie's arm, her voice softening. "And I didn't mean to snap at you, Gertie. It's just that, well, things feel all mixed up to me right now." Picking up the heaping plate of cookies, she began to head out to the front room.

"Love'll do that to you," Gertie murmured under her breath.

Hannah stopped in the doorway, turning her head. "What did you say?"

"Not enough sleep'll do that to you," Gertie replied innocently. Picking up the second platter Hannah had prepared, Gertie followed her out. "Tonight, why not let me stay here and you go to my house? Nice and peaceful there," she promised. "Nobody'll disturb you—unless you want them to, of course."

Gertie placed the platter on the table against the wall, leaving it to Penny Sue to distribute the cookies. Squeals and pleas immediately abounded from the pint-sized citizenry.

Moving aside, Hannah lowered her voice as she inclined her head next to Gertie's ear. "I don't see what you're doing, volunteering in a daycare center, Gertie. You should be running a matchmaking service."

Gertie pursed her lips together, eyeing Hannah purposely. "Don't seem to be having much luck in that department right now."

She looked at the slender young blond doctor in the front room, who, along with Penny Sue and Gwenyth, was suddenly inundated by a sea of little hands, all raised for hand-outs. New to Storkville, the woman had offered her services to the center in the last few weeks, despite a full-time career and home.

"I'm hoping for better luck with my lemonade. Well, not me, exactly." Gertie lowered her voice to a whisper. "But Dr. Becky. Made up a batch just for her this morning. That don't do the trick, I'm afraid nothing will."

Hannah looked at the woman they were talking about. Dr. Becky was Dr. Rebecca Fielding who, together with her husband, Dr. Mike Fielding, worked at Storkville General Hospital. Rebecca had been attempting to become pregnant for over a year now. The irony of it was that Rebecca was an ob/gyn, up on the latest fertility breakthroughs.

Frustrated and desperate at not finding herself in the family way each month, it looked as if she was about to subscribe to Aunt Gertie's theory that her "special, top-secret lemonade"—which Gertie had announced was "patent pending"—would do the trick where science and the machinations of simple human nature had failed.

Maybe Becky was merely humoring Gertie, Hannah thought. "Has she had any yet?"

"She says she's thinking about it, but I think she's weakening. Poor lamb, I can see it in her eyes every time she comes here." Gertie sighed, watching Becky distribute cookies to gleeful takers. "She wants babies something awful." Gertie glanced at Hannah. "Seems to be a lot of that going on lately."

Hannah took no offense at Gertie's implication. Here, at least, the older woman was right. "Well, for all intents and purposes, I have babies. Two babies." She looked toward where the twins were sitting in their infant seats jabbering away to one another in babyspeak. She could have watched them for hours.

"Indefinitely if their mother or father doesn't come back to claim them."

And right now, that wasn't looking like such a bad thing, Hannah thought. It did no good to try to distance herself from the twins in case Tucker was successful in his efforts to track down their mother. The twosome had already bagged her heart as a trophy. To pretend otherwise would have been a useless lie.

"Even if they do, it'll be a while before they can take custody of the twins," Gertie pointed out. "Mom and/or dad will be facing jail time."

If this were one of the larger cities, there would be no question of that. But people tended to be more forgiving in Storkville, Hannah thought.

"Oh, I've got a feeling Tucker might find a way around that if they turn out to be really contrite."

Gertie shook her head. "I don't know about that. Tucker's pretty hard on things like abandonment. It's no secret he believes that people should face up to their responsibilities. He's got a lot in common with Jackson there."

There was no need to praise Jackson to her. Hannah already thought of him as being in the same realm as a white knight. But she didn't quite grasp what Gertie was trying to say. "How so?"

To keep from being overheard, Gertie stepped out into the foyer. "Well, he came back, didn't he? To take care of his daddy's funeral. The way that boy lit out of town when he left, I didn't think he was ever coming back."

Hannah stared at the older woman. She'd never had any details about that day, only that somewhere during the course of the reception, Jackson had taken off.

It was only later that evening, as she and Ethan were leaving on their honeymoon, that she'd heard Jackson had not just left the reception, but the town as well.

"You saw him leave?"

"Yes, I saw him leave. Nearly ran me down with that car of his. Of course, I don't think he saw me. But I saw him, just for a second when the car drove by. He looked really upset." Gertie sighed and shook her head. "I always figured he and his daddy had had some kind of a major falling-out. Things were never the same between those two after his Momma died of a heart attack."

Hannah remembered how distraught Jackson had been. She'd never seen him that way before. There had been only a momentary break in the strong front he always presented to the world, but she had seen it. Seen the tears brimming in Jackson's eyes. Though he hadn't seemed particularly close to his mother, her death had hit him hard. Anna Caldwell had died alone in her room. Rumor had it that her husband was out on the town. Jackson had been the one to discover her when he came in to say good-night.

Hannah had done her best to comfort him, had been by his side at the funeral but there'd been no reaching Jackson. He'd gone off into that place he went to whenever he wanted to distance himself from what was going on around him.

She'd ached for him that day. And later.

"But he came back to tie up all the loose ends, make whatever amends he had to," Gertie concluded. "That makes him a big man in my book."

Hannah didn't understand. "Amends?"

"For his daddy. That man was always tomcatting

around. Those two might have shared a name, but they're nothing alike. Jackson's daddy was a charmer and as shallow as a one-inch pool. Our doctor-boy might not smile much, but he runs deep. And he's got a good heart.'' She looked at Hannah pointedly. ''Remember that.''

Hannah saw no reason for the advice. ''I do.''

''Good.'' Gertie suddenly smiled broadly. ''Because it looks like he's back.'' She pointed to the front door.

Chapter Seven

Still holding the platter of cookies, Hannah turned around to open the door with her free hand, then stepped back to allow Jackson to come in. The grandfather clock in the study chimed the hour. It was two. He was late.

"I thought maybe you weren't coming today," she told him as she closed the door.

"I almost didn't."

Gertie's words rang in her ear. He'd realized that there was no further need to keep coming this way and was about to tell her this was the last time. She braced herself. "Oh?"

"There was an emergency at the office. At least, Mrs. Donovan thought it was an emergency. Her son Teddy decided he liked pussy willows so much, he stuck them up his nose to keep them close forever. According to Mrs. Donovan, he started screaming almost immediately.'' Jackson shook his head. "Tucker escorted her and Teddy into the office.''

"Why?'' Hannah wouldn't have thought that pussy willows would readily come under the heading of a 911 call for the sheriff.

"Seems Mrs. Donovan ran every light from her house to my office, thinking Teddy was going to choke to death.'' The woman was lucky to have made it to his office without causing an accident, he thought.

Acquainted with the two, Hannah could just envision it. Jackson, in the eye of a hurricane, trying to calmly go about his work while Mrs. Donovan wrung her hands, lamenting, and her son screamed blue murder. "So I take it that you successfully separated Teddy from the pussy willows?''

"Not without much protest.'' He tugged on his ear. "My ears are still ringing. I tell you, if that kid doesn't become either an opera singer or an umpire, then it'll be a great loss to one world or the other.'' For the first time, he became aware of the plate she was holding. Oatmeal chocolate chip had always been his favorite and time had done nothing to alter that fact. He could feel his taste buds go into high gear. "Anyway, can I convince you to give me one of those?''

The way he looked at the cookies on the plate had her suddenly wishing she was one, too. "You're in luck. I'm highly bribable today.''

The smile that curved his lips was nothing short of powerfully sexy. "What'll you take in trade?''

Silently, she offered one to him, and he made it his own immediately. Hannah watched as he bit into the cookie with the relish of a small boy who'd managed to break into a secret hiding place and appropriated the booty. There was contented pleasure in Jackson's expression.

Was it possible to be envious of a cookie? she wondered.

"A little adult conversation that doesn't have 'like' appearing twice in every sentence, or that ends in some thinly veiled innuendo that I should start thinking about becoming the nineties, updated version of The Merry Widow. That's an operetta," she added in case he missed the reference.

The last of the large cookie disappeared between his lips. He eyed her. "Hannah Dawson, are you talking down to me?"

Dawson. He was the second person to call her that today. Hannah realized that hearing her maiden name seemed far more appropriate to her than hearing her married one. Funny, now that she thought of it, but she felt far more like Hannah Dawson these days than Hannah Brady. She wasn't even sure just how Hannah Brady would feel anymore. It was almost a relief to put Hannah Brady behind her now.

"Talk down to you?" she echoed. "I wouldn't dream of it. It's just that most men aren't familiar enough with operettas and old musicals to even recognize their names."

He pinched a second cookie, his eyes shining. "I recognize it. And if that's your way of saying I'm unique. I'll accept it."

Leaning against the wall, she knew she could stand like this with him forever. They were talking almost

PLAY THE
Lucky Key Game
and get

HOW TO PLAY:

1. With a coin, carefully scratch off gold area at the right. Then check the claim chart to see what we have for you — **2 FREE BOOKS** and a **FREE GIFT** — **ALL YOURS FREE!**

2. Send back the card and you'll receive two brand-new Silhouette Romance® novels. These books have a cover price of $3.50 each in the U.S. and $3.99 each in Canada, but they are yours to keep absolutely free.

3. There's no catch. You're under no obligation to buy anything. We charge nothing —ZERO — for your first shipment. And you don't have to make any minimum number of purchases — not even one!

4. The fact is, thousands of readers enjoy receiving books by mail from the Silhouette Reader Service™. They enjoy the convenience of home delivery...they like getting the best new novels at discount prices, **BEFORE** they're available in stores...and they love their *Heart to Heart* subscriber newsletter featuring author news, horoscopes, recipes, book reviews and much more!

5. We hope that after receiving your free books you'll want to remain a subscriber. But the choice is yours — to continue or cancel, any time at all! So why not take us up on our invitation, with no risk of any kind. You'll be glad you did!

YOURS FREE!
A SURPRISE MYSTERY GIFT

We can't tell you what it is...but we're sure you'll like it! A
FREE GIFT—
just for playing the
LUCKY KEY game!

**Visit us online at
www.eHarlequin.com**

FREE GIFTS!

NO COST! NO OBLIGATION TO BUY!
NO PURCHASE NECESSARY!

PLAY THE
Lucky Key Game

Scratch gold area with a coin.
Then check below to see the gifts you get!

315 SDL C4FJ
215 SDL C4FE

YES! I have scratched off the gold area. Please send me the 2 Free books and gift for which I qualify. I understand I am under no obligation to purchase any books, as explained on the back and on the opposite page.

NAME (PLEASE PRINT CLEARLY)

ADDRESS

APT.# CITY

STATE/PROV. ZIP/POSTAL CODE

2 free books plus a mystery gift

2 free books

1 free book

Try Again!

Offer limited to one per household and not valid to current Silhouette Romance® subscribers. All orders subject to approval.

(S-R-OS-08/00)

The Silhouette Reader Service™ — Here's how it works:

Accepting your 2 free books and gift places you under no obligation to buy anything. You may keep the books and gift and return the shipping statement marked "cancel." If you do not cancel, about a month later we'll send you 6 additional novels and bill you just $2.90 each in the U.S., or $3.25 each in Canada, plus 25¢ delivery per book and applicable taxes if any.*
That's the complete price and — compared to cover prices of $3.50 each in the U.S. and $3.99 each in Canada — it's quite a bargain! You may cancel at any time, but if you choose to continue, every month we'll send you 6 more books, which you may either purchase at the discount price or return to us and cancel your subscription.

*Terms and prices subject to change without notice. Sales tax applicable in N.Y. Canadian residents will be charged applicable provincial taxes and GST.

like the old days. Days she missed acutely. "Fishing for a compliment, are we?"

Since she seemed to be in a good mood, he availed himself of one more cookie. After all, lunch had come and gone and his stomach was still empty.

"It's been a hard morning. Dana Hewitt brought her triplets in for their check ups. Unfortunately, the visit also included boosters." There were times when being a pediatrician was a challenge. This had been one of those times. He'd needed the extra hands of not only the triplet's mother, but of his nurse as well. "You think twins are a handful, take it from me, they've got nothing on triplets. That woman deserves a medal."

If the last week was any indication of what Dana Hewitt's life was like, Hannah had another take on the assessment. "I'm sure she'd enjoy a mini-vacation instead."

"You're probably right," he agreed. "These are good." Jackson held up the tiny piece he had left of his third cookie. "You make them?"

She shook her head, straightening. "Wish I could take the credit. No, that's just one the talents that Gertie brings with her to the place."

Moving slightly back, she caught sight of Gertie: she was playing a board game with three of the older children. A fond smile slipped over Hannah's lips as she watched for a moment.

"She gossips like a supermarket tabloid at times, but her heart's in the right place and I know I'd be lost without her. We've only been open for a few weeks and she's already indispensable to me." Hannah sighed, grappling with reality. "I just wish I could pay her."

"Oh, I think she's getting compensated," he assured Hannah, observing the older woman. Judging by the wide grin, Gertie was having the time of her life. "Kids might run you ragged, but they keep you young and moving."

A rubber ball came flying at them out of nowhere. Hannah's hand whipped out, making the catch before the ball could hit her.

"Yeah, to avoid being a target." Pulling her face into a serious expression, purely to get her point across, she looked at the two culprits who had come running up to her for their ball. Rather than surrendering it, she rhythmically tossed it up in the air and then caught it. "Boys, what did I tell you about playing ball in the house?"

"Don't," they both chimed in together.

"Right. Take it outside." She handed the ball to the child closest to her, a tow-headed boy of four named Neil. "And you," she said, looking at Jackson, "why don't you take it inside?"

Frowning, he looked about elaborately. "I thought I was inside."

"I mean into the parlor." She nodded toward the room where her great-aunt used to entertain suitors as a young woman under her father's watchful eye. "Sit down a few minutes, take a deep breath." She looked at what he was still holding in his hand. "Enjoy your cookie."

Her words amused him. "Trying your hand at playing doctor?"

"No, just being head of a daycare center. Giving

orders seems to come with the territory.'' So did having eyes in the back of your head, she thought. Turning, she made eye contact with Ricky Fellows and shook her head. He let go of Lily Allen's braid, a contrite expression on his young face. Lily ran off.

She did have a way about her, Jackson thought. She was far more authoritative than he'd ever thought her capable of being. ''I notice that no one seems to mind listening to you.''

''Being taller than all of them has its advantages.'' She laughed to herself. ''I can remember when I thought being tall was the most awful thing that could have happened to me.'' Feelings vividly replayed themselves in her mind. ''I felt like such a beanpole.''

He'd never thought of her as awkward or gangly. ''You were striking.''

The euphemism made her laugh softly. ''Yeah, easy for you to say now. Where were you when I could have used someone to back me up?''

To him, Hannah had always been able to handle herself. He could never have played Lancelot to her damsel in distress. She wouldn't have expected it or tolerated it. ''I don't recall you ever needing any backup.''

A lot he knew. She'd been teased a great deal, but she had pretended to have a tough skin. Eventually, the teasing had stopped. Blossoming the way she had hadn't hurt, either.

''That was because you were too surrounded with sweet, young, overly nubile things to be able to see past the tight circle they formed around you.''

When had she learned to exaggerate? ''Funny, I don't seem to recall your imagination being so creative.'' He looked down at the plate she was still holding. When had he managed to eat so many cookies? ''I seem to have depleted your supply.''

''There's more in the front room, if you want to risk venturing in.'' He raised his brow, puzzled. ''The kids have all had their naps and, thanks to Gertie, their afternoon sugar high,'' Hannah explained. ''They should be fairly ready to bounce off all the walls by now.''

''The way around that,'' he told her, walking into the room and straight for the other plate, ''is to get them into some calm group activity. Read them a story.''

That was all the rabble had to hear, Hannah thought, looking at them fondly. Prior activities and even the cookies were forgotten at the mention of their favorite word.

''A story?'' Jonathan, a tiny, freckled boy piped up, excitement lacing his high voice.

Suddenly, the cry of ''Story, story,'' went up all over the room. Before he knew what was happening, Jackson found himself beset by almost a dozen up-turned faces, all eagerly looking at him.

From the center of the pint-sized ring, Jackson turned toward Hannah. He could hear Penny Sue and Becky laughing on the sidelines. ''I take it that's the wrong word to use around here.''

''Depends on who you are.'' Hannah stepped forward to rescue him. ''Maybe you'd better pocket a few more cookies and make your escape while you can. I'll take it from here. The babies are in the next room, still down for their naps.''

But Jackson was in no hurry to get away. He enjoyed reading to children. "That's okay, I've got a little time before I have to get back. My next two appointments canceled. I can read a story as long as it's not too long."

There were children's books of all lengths, thanks to the library Hannah's great-aunt had maintained. She looked through a few that were on the table. "How are you with Dr. Seuss?"

Jackson held out his hand for the book. "Just my speed."

She sincerely doubted that. The man went far beyond the elementary and endearing words found between the covers of the children's favorite author. Selecting one of the late writer's more popular books, she gave it to Jackson then sat back and waited to hear him read.

Pleasant surprise arrived almost instantly.

It was hard to reconcile the wild, brooding bad boy she'd once secretly pressed to her heart with the dark-haired man who now sat cross-legged on the floor, surrounded by an enthralled audience hanging on his every word, even though those words had been all but memorized by the same audience.

He'd chosen the right profession, Hannah thought, watching him. Children were intuitive, they could sense who liked them and who was only pretending. There was no pretense with Jackson Caldwell. Anyone could see that he liked children; liked not only the idea of children, but the reality of them as well: the demands children could make so easily on his time and patience.

Jackson read to them with gusto and feeling, his

voice taking on the nature of the characters in the book.

He didn't merely read, he performed, Hannah noted. And the children ate it up with glee.

"More," they cried almost in unison when he closed the book, adding a heart twisting "pleeease," before he could turn them down.

Rising, Jackson looked to her for help. The single telegraphed plea went right through her, warming Hannah. She liked the fact that for this single instant, she and Jackson were a team.

"Dr. Caldwell has to go back to his office right now, kids. But I'm sure he'll be back again very soon if you all behave yourselves." Grasping him by the wrist, Hannah extricated him from his admirers, then accompanied him out to the foyer.

"Nicely done, especially that behave part." He found himself smiling into her eyes when she turned to face him at the door. Smiling into them and getting lost there. "Don't miss a trick, do you?"

She wouldn't have quite put it that way, but she was glad that he had. "I might be taller, but they definitely outnumber me. I can't afford to let them get the upper hand."

He was almost to the door when he remembered why he'd come in the first place. "I almost forgot, how are the twins today?"

There was really no need for him to examine either of the two. They were healthy and thriving. "Getting cuter every day. Steffie's over her cold and Sammy's not showing any signs that he's coming down with it. I don't think he caught it." A wave of sadness washed over her. Hannah hid it, slipping her hands into her pockets. "I guess that means you won't have to be stopping by anymore."

When she looked like that, she almost seemed vulnerable. "I didn't just come by to look in on the twins."

"Oh, really?" She knew she shouldn't be holding her breath. But she was.

"Really," he echoed. "I needed to spend some time with an old friend."

She told herself this wasn't ever going to go past this stage and that it should be enough. "Watch the old part. I'm sensitive."

"You're also as far from being old as I am from being a leprechaun."

"Well, that's because they have a height requirement."

He snapped his fingers. "There you go, dashing my hopes again."

"Again?" She thought she saw a fleeting, wary look in his eyes when she asked. But the next moment, it was gone and she told herself she'd just imagined it.

"Poetic license. Listen, can you get a sitter for the twins tonight?"

She thought of Gwenyth, but her cousin was busy going between her house and the one Gwenyth was about to rent, getting it ready. She didn't want to impose on her. "There's Gertie. She keeps volunteering to stay with them. Why? What did you have in mind?"

"Nothing much, just a sudden whim for dinner away from the madding crowd. Maybe catch a movie. The way we did in the old days."

In the old days, she recalled, there were three of them doing things together. Even after she and Ethan had gotten engaged.

"You're on," she told him.

He almost called twice to cancel, upbraiding himself in the confines of his own mind all afternoon and on the drive back to his house. It was a mistake to go through with this. Seeing her at the daycare center with a score or so of children and adults within several inches of them at any given time was one thing, an intimate table for two was quite another.

"What the hell were you thinking of?" he asked himself.

What he'd been thinking of was having dinner with a beautiful woman. Of isolating an evening and pretending, just for a while, that actions had no consequences, no ripple effects, and that he had no shadows cast over him, no heritage weighing heavily on him.

Would it be so hard, he wondered, to let himself pretend? Just this once?

He was still carrying on the terse, if silent argument as he drove over to Hannah's home.

Time to stop arguing, he told himself, turning the ignition off. He was here.

Jackson took a deep breath, then opened his door and got out.

This was ridiculous. He didn't recall ever being nervous about taking a woman out before. But then, he'd never taken Hannah out before, at least, not alone. Oh, there had been long, one-on-one talks and evenings spent in each other's company, but then there had usually been a schoolbook in between them, sparking the initial reason for the get-together.

Never, in all those years, had he approached her door with the intention of taking her out for the evening without Ethan being somewhere very close by.

Confidence was a wonderful thing, he thought as he walked away from his car. You only realized how much you needed it when it was absent.

Calling himself an idiot, Jackson made himself go up the front steps before he changed his mind and chalked the whole venture up to a bad idea that should have never been executed.

Even if he went through with it, there certainly was no future to it beyond tonight.

He wasn't sure if that knowledge relieved him, or made him sad.

This was Hannah, he told himself. Hannah, whose company he enjoyed. Hannah, who had been a part of everything in his life that had been good and clean and decent. When the ugliness in his own home had threatened to overwhelm him, when he couldn't bear to be privy to the lies, the deceit that went on behind the walls of the Caldwell estate, he would seek out Hannah, Hannah and her parents, who had both been so normal, so warm. Being part of their lives had reminded him that the world wasn't completely bathed in dark hues, that there were good people around and that men could stay faithful to wives who loved them.

She was part of the light and he was part of the dark, he thought as he rang the doorbell, listening to the soft chimes. There could be no future because he wouldn't allow himself to taint that light. But for tonight, there could be a present.

He strained to hear approaching footsteps from somewhere beyond the other side of the door.

Hearing the doorbell, Gertie went to the foot of the stairs and called up, "Jackson's here. Don't keep him waiting, dear."

Nerves suddenly popped out, as huge as stealth bombers and moving just as swiftly through Hannah.

Could you will the flu? Or a fever? Hannah wondered, looking herself over in the full length mirror and seeing only disaster.

Because if she could will herself instantly ill, she wanted to. Desperately. Every outfit she owned had been tried on and discarded, deemed all wrong for the occasion. She literally had nothing to wear and she didn't want to go.

Didn't want to be disappointed.

Get on with it, Hannah, she ordered herself.

Hurriedly Hannah slipped into shoes that matched her dress and grabbed her purse off her bed.

The walk to the head of the stairs felt as if she were taking the last mile. Gertie was down there, waiting. The doorbell rang again and Gertie looked up at her expectantly.

Hannah took a deep breath and then let it out again before coming down. "I thought in your generation you were supposed to keep a man waiting."

Gertie snorted. "My generation had a few things backwards. And besides, you've already kept him waiting for a long time, wouldn't you say?"

"What I'd say," Hannah told her, stopping to kiss

the wrinkled pink cheek for luck as well as out of affection, "is that you've been inhaling too much talcum powder lately and it's made your thinking fuzzy. Jackson and I are just friends."

Gertie nodded, stopping a second to fuss with a tendril at Hannah's temple. "Friendship is a very important ingredient in the mix and a good place to start. Well, go on," Gertie waved her to the door, "let him in."

Hannah felt as if she were using someone else's legs as she crossed to the door and finally opened it. Someone else's voice came out of her mouth. "Hi."

He'd begun to think he'd gotten his nights mixed up and that she wasn't home. Seeing her now froze all thoughts in his head. She was wearing a simple electric-blue sheath that caressed every curve on her body.

And made him want to do the same.

There was barely enough saliva in his mouth for him to offer a single word in reply. "Wow."

She couldn't read his expression. "Is that a good wow or a bad wow?"

"A good wow. Definitely a very good wow." He raised his eyes to her face, then tilted his head. "What have you done to your hair?"

She *knew* she should have left it down. "You don't like it?" She was already grasping at a pin. "I can take it down—"

Jackson caught her wrist gently in his hand. "No, I like it. I like it very much."

There was something in the way he looked at her that made her body feel warm all over.

Hannah nearly melted as Jackson took her wrap from her and slid it up along her arms.

Finding her voice, she turned to look at Gertie. "Thanks for watching the twins. I'll be home early."

"I won't hold you to that," Gertie called after her. "Have a good time!"

"We will," Jackson tossed over his shoulder, slipping his arm around Hannah's as he ushered her down the porch steps.

Embarrassment harnessed her. Could Gertie have been any more obvious?

"Are my cheeks red?" Hannah asked him.

Stopping at the passenger side of his vehicle, he pretended to take a closer look at her face, then laughed. "Only very pleasantly so."

The sound of his laugh helped quell the uneasiness in her stomach.

But not much.

Chapter Eight

Hannah felt his eyes on her. When she raised her own to his, she realized that he wasn't looking at her, he was looking at her plate.

Jackson frowned. She'd hardly touched anything. "I don't remember you eating like a bird."

It wasn't that the food wasn't good, it was just that the knot in her stomach wouldn't loosen enough to let her enjoy it. Telling herself that she was acting like an idiot didn't help.

She grasped at diversion. "Actually, that's a misconception. Depending on the bird, they can eat up to three or four times their weight a day."

Taking a sip of his wine, Jackson laughed, shaking his head. "That part I remember."

Just to the right of them, the band began to play a low, bluesy number and she began tapping her foot to the rhythm. "What? About the birds?"

"No, about you correcting me. You did that a lot

when we were growing up." She'd been fearless like that, he remembered, never allowing him to labor under a misconception when she could help it. He grinned. "I guess your mother never told you that correcting a guy when he's wrong might damage his ego."

She raised her own glass and took a small sip of wine. It felt as if it was going straight to her head. Or was that him? "From where I sit, your ego's fine, and my mother taught me to be myself."

He wouldn't have had it any other way. It was what had always made Hannah so unique to him. She'd always had the courage of her convictions, never standing on ceremony, but doing and saying what she thought was right.

"Smart lady, your mother. I always liked your parents." They had died six months apart and he'd missed both their funerals, not having heard about their deaths until it had been far too late even to send condolences. He leaned forward over the table. "How have you held up since they…?"

A vague shrug rippled along her shoulders. Losing them had been far harder for her to deal with than Ethan's death. "As well as can be expected. Not a day goes by when I don't miss them."

He could well understand that. "At least you had them."

"You had yours, too."

He set his mouth grimly. "Not the same thing." He'd never been close to his parents, not even his mother, whom he'd loved. There'd never been a feeling of unity, as he'd observed in hers. "My parents weren't like yours. Yours were warm-hearted people.''

She knew his parents was a sore topic for him so she left it alone. ''They liked you, too.''

He warmed to the memories, letting them in. He'd hung around her house so much, the Dawsons had all but adopted him as the son they'd never had. He supposed, looking back, he'd sought emotional asylum with them.

''What I liked most about your parents was that they were honest and real. There were no pretenses, no hidden secrets. Every time your father looked at your mother, I knew he was in love with her.'' How many times had he wished Hannah's father had been his own? Too many to begin to remember. ''That's a very rare quality in a man.''

She thought of Ethan. ''I know. At least in some men.''

He looked at her for a long moment, wondering if she was thinking of him when she said that. Jackson nodded at her neglected plate. ''Well, since you're not eating, would you like to dance?''

She stopped tapping her toe and stared at Jackson. ''Now?''

He grinned at the surprise in her eyes. ''Since the band's here and they're playing I thought that now might not be a bad time, yes.''

In all the time she'd known him, he'd never asked her to dance. Not that she hadn't fantasized about it countless times. But right now, she wasn't sure that she could. ''You're asking me to dance with you?''

''Am I not speaking English?'' he asked with a laugh.

She shook her head as if to clear it, not as if she were giving him a silent answer.

"I'm sorry, it's just that—" She stopped, collecting herself. Since he liked honesty so much, she decided to give it a try and tell him why she was stuttering like some confused, adolescent schoolgirl. "You have no idea how many times I used to imagine that you'd ask me to dance."

"Used to?"

In for a penny, in for a pound, wasn't that what her great-aunt used to say? Hannah nodded. "Yes."

"When?"

Lowering her eyes, she looked at the way the light was squeezing itself through the wine in her glass and twinkling over the surface. "When we were growing up. You want me to give you inclusive dates?"

Was she serious? How could he have missed that? Missed the implication behind it? "No, it's just that I had no idea…"

She raised her eyes. "You didn't have an idea about a lot of things."

Just how far did this lead? he wondered. Had she cared for him once as something more than just a friend? "Such as?"

"Such as the way girls felt about you." Hannah bit her lip, then let the words free. "And the way I felt about you."

"You."

"Me."

He still couldn't get himself to believe it. Hannah had to mean something else, there had to be something qualifying her words to keep them from meaning what he thought they meant. "And that was…?"

She'd just reached the end of her embarrassment tether. Nervous, she forced herself to stop twirling the stem of her wine glass between her fingers. "What is this, you buy a girl a little dinner, ply her with wine and then expect her to give you all her secrets?"

He didn't want her to feel as if he were probing, pushing her. She probably thought he was doing it to have his vanity stroked when nothing could have been further from the truth. To spare her, despite his desire to know, he withdrew. "I didn't mean—"

Hannah moved back her chair and let him guide her to the dance floor. She couldn't leave him wondering, but she could couch it in the past, saving her own face. "Well, all right, I guess you're entitled to know. You would have known if you'd only been paying attention. I had the biggest secret crush on you."

Crush, Hannah figured, was a far safer word than *love,* though the latter was much closer to the truth than the former.

And still is, a voice whispered across her mind.

"You did." It was more of a stunned repetition than a question.

He looked, she thought, as if he could be knocked over with the proverbial feather. Or maybe he'd just gone into shock. She didn't know whether to be amused or hurt. "I did."

He didn't know what to think, what to say. "And was it?"

She didn't follow. "Was it what?"

"A secret?" Or had she told someone? Had she shared her feelings with someone else and made it seem as if he were some heartless idiot who ignored her? God, but he wished he had known, had some inkling.

Was he worried that she might have embarrassed him by sharing her feelings for him with a girlfriend? "I never told anyone how I felt, if that's what you mean." The smile that found its way to her lips never reached her eyes. "Only my diary knew."

Something else he didn't know about her, he thought. How much more was there that had eluded him? "You kept a diary?"

"Sure." She'd kept one faithfully during her teen years and into her twenties. She'd stopped the day before she married Ethan. Looking back, she wondered if that had been some sort of sign she'd ignored. "I had to get my feelings out somehow—or bust."

The conversation was getting serious, and awkward. He made an attempt to lighten it for both their sakes. "I thought you always took your feelings out on Ethan and me—but I guess I was wrong."

She looked at him for a long moment. "Yeah, you were. About a lot of things."

When he'd opened the door with what he'd thought was a harmless question, he hadn't been prepared for the flood of revelations that came his way. But he couldn't help asking, "Meaning?"

She might as well clear the air about as much as she could. But she would keep back the most important part. "Leaving town like that, in the middle of our wedding. Gertie seemed to think that it was because of some argument you had with your father. Was it?"

He had no idea how Gertie could have had an opinion about his departure, one way or another. Gossip, he supposed. But gossip wasn't what he wanted Hannah to know. "No, by then my father and I weren't really speaking. He was into his own thing and hardly knew that I was alive. I don't think he even realized I'd left for several weeks." By then he'd long since moved out of the house and taken a place near the hospital. "It wasn't as if we ran into each other a lot. He was busy elsewhere."

Tom-catting around, Gertie had called it, Hannah thought. But she wasn't about to open up wounds that might not have completely healed. "All right, if you didn't leave because of your father, why did you leave?"

He didn't want to go into that. Not yet, perhaps not ever. He nodded toward the band. "The music's stopped."

But she remained where she was for a moment, looking at him. "So have the answers."

"Let it alone, Hannah." Placing his hand to the small of her back, he ushered her back to their table. "It doesn't concern you."

Stunned and momentarily speechless she blew out an angry breath as she sank down in her seat again. "Well, I guess that certainly puts me in my place, doesn't it?"

Words had never been his best method of communication. "Hey, I didn't mean—"

Hannah cut him off, not wanting to hear any lies. "Didn't you? You tell me that we're friends, and then you tell me to butt out. Is there some kind of tier arrangement you have for your friends, a caste system I wasn't aware of?"

Telling her the truth might kill the very friendship she was throwing in his face. "Hannah—"

Living with Ethan had taught her how to withdraw into her shell. "Sorry, maybe I expected too much. Maybe I just expected you to be honest with me." A flood of emotions threatened to drown her. She could feel them welling up inside. "But if Ethan couldn't be, why should you? You owe me less than he did."

The conversation was swiftly going in directions he didn't follow. "Ethan? What are you talking about? What wasn't Ethan honest about?"

She'd said too much, alluded to too much and she could feel tears beginning to sting her eyes. She wanted to leave before he could see them. Taking her purse, she rose abruptly. "Look, it's been a lovely evening, but I really have to go."

Before he could say anything, she hurried away.

He caught up to Hannah in the parking lot. There was no way he was going to let her leave like this, with so much hanging unspoken between them. Catching her by the arm, he turned her around to face him, fighting to curb the flash of temper he felt. "Just where do you think you're going?"

Stubbornly, she tried to pull her arm away, but he had a firm hold on it. "Home."

His eyes narrowed. "On foot?"

Hannah tossed her head. "We still have buses here. We're not entirely backward, no matter what you might think."

"Nobody ever said you were backward."

"Then why treat me that way?" Hannah demanded, finally managing to pull herself free. "Why not answer me?"

"Because you might not like the answers."

Some of the anger left her voice, softening it. "Why don't you let me decide that?"

He couldn't risk it. Couldn't tear away the one good, decent thing that had been part of his life. That was why he had left to begin with, because he was afraid that jealousy would get the better of him, outweighing his friendship.

"Because it wouldn't be fair to you. It's bad enough that…"

She waited for him to continue, but he didn't. "That what?"

He only shook his head. Confession was not always good for the soul. Sometimes, it hurt more than it healed. "Never mind."

She knew defeat when she faced it and her frustration was hard to contain. "There you go again, keeping things from me. Is it a thing with you men?"

She was still talking in riddles, riddles he intended to solve. If there was something troubling her, he wanted to know. No one was more important to him than Hannah. "What are you talking about? And what was it about Ethan you wouldn't tell me back there?"

He noticed that they were garnering curious glances from a couple just leaving their car. Taking her by the arm, he began to walk to the edge of the parking lot, as calmly as if they were out for a stroll instead of trying to resolve something between them.

She looked for words that wouldn't come. "I don't want to tell you because you and Ethan were friends and because…because I couldn't stand it if you thought there was nothing wrong with it." What if he took Ethan's side? What if he told her that all men cheated on their wives and that it was something to turn a blind eye to?

He was more lost than ever—and more determined to find his way. "Start at the beginning."

Where was the beginning? Did she even remember anymore? Hannah thought. "I can't. I don't know when the beginning was. It just sort of started."

They had left the restaurant lot and were walking along the block, the way they used to. Except the topics had never been so serious then. "What just sort of started?"

"Ethan's stepping out on me."

Jackson stopped walking and looked at her. "What?"

"Stepping out on me. Seeing other women. Betraying our vows. I don't know how else to say it. I don't want to say it," she cried. "It tastes too bitter on my tongue to have to talk about it."

Of all the things she could have said, this was something he wouldn't have guessed. Ethan had been crazy about Hannah. It was one of the reasons Jackson had stepped away, because he was so certain that Ethan would love her the way she deserved to be loved. The way her father had loved her mother.

Jackson felt a sense of betrayal, for her as well as for his own beliefs. "Ethan saw other women?"

She laughed shortly and began walking again. "I see you still have that razor-sharp mind of yours."

"When?" Jackson still couldn't make himself believe it. "When was he seeing other women?" Maybe it had only been her imagination, he thought. But he had never known her to be the suspicious type.

"When wasn't he? I'd like to think that the honeymoon was free of other women, but I can't really swear to that. I suppose he might have caught a lady or two on the side even then. Hawaii was full of beautiful women and I was too busy getting used to the idea that it was only the two of us from there on in." Hannah glanced at him pointedly, the streetlight illuminating the sadness in her eyes.

It still seemed so unreal to him. "Ethan? Ethan cheated on you?"

Why couldn't he accept it? She had. And then the fear began to form within her again. Was he going to blame her for Ethan's indiscretions? Was he going ask if she drove him to it? If she wasn't woman enough for Ethan?

She couldn't help the sarcasm that entered her voice. "With every breath he took, I eventually discovered. I tried to pretend it wasn't happening, tried to act like the good little wife and make him happy but it seemed that what really made Ethan happy was variety."

Words couldn't begin to explain how angry he felt for her. "Oh God, Hannah, I'm so sorry."

"Yeah, me, too," she said softly. "Did you know that when he died there was someone else in the car with him? He'd told me he was going out of town on business. Tucker tried to hide it from me. I guess he figured I was going through enough without having that tidbit thrown at me. But I found out." She pushed the hurt away as best she could. "The wife always finds out, you know. And usually sooner than later."

Because he had no words to tell her how sorry he was, no words to express how truly surprised he was, Jackson said nothing. But he took Hannah into his arms and just held her. Held her as a friend, not as someone who had loved her in silence.

He blamed himself for what she'd gone through. The irony of it twisted through him like a sharp knife. He'd tried to spare her and because he had pushed her into Ethan's arms, Hannah had endured the very thing he'd been trying to prevent.

"I'm getting your jacket all wet," she said.

"It'll dry."

He took out a handkerchief from his pocket and slowly dried her eyes with it. She held very still.

"I really needed you back then," Hannah whispered. "I needed someone to talk to. I wished you had left me a number, an address, something."

Pocketing the handkerchief again, he threaded his fingers through hers. They started to walk again. "I'm sorry, so very sorry, Hannah."

"I know." She did. She just needed to hear him say it. "No point in dredging up the past this way. It's done and gone."

They'd walked full circle, coming back to the restaurant's parking lot. He nodded toward it. "Want to go back and finish our meal?"

"You think it's still there?" They'd been walking for at least fifteen minutes. "They've probably cleared the table by now."

"Only one way to find out." Jackson put his hand out to her.

After a moment's hesitation, Hannah placed her hand into it. "I guess I'm game if you are."

The table, they discovered, was still just as they left it. Their server had obviously thought they were still on the dance floor. When they walked past him from the direction of the front entrance, he looked at them oddly. Waiting until they were seated, he approached and asked if they wanted something else instead.

"Just dessert," Jackson said, then looked at Hannah. "Unless you—"

The knot that had been in her stomach had shrunk some. Enough to slide in a rich piece of cake, or at least ice cream.

"Dessert sounds fine." She gave the server her order, then waited until he retreated after writing down Jackson's choice. "You still have that sweet tooth?"

"What?" He laughed. When he was a kid, he'd always felt that meals should begin with dessert and if there was any room left over, then something healthy should be added. As a doctor, he was forced, at least in theory, to reverse his preference. "Eating Gertie's cookies didn't convince you?"

"I guess you do at that." She thought of the unexpected afternoon treat. "The kids loved having you there today, reading to them. I'd forgotten how much patience you had."

The server returned with a giant slice of cake that would have confounded a lesser man. Jackson merely looked at it with relish. "What do you mean?"

She raised her long spoon and began diminishing the sundae that had been placed before her. "That semester you tried to teach me calculus."

"Oh, yeah. As I remember it, I didn't try. I succeeded."

"Only after long, harrowing hours." Perhaps a little longer than was truly necessary, but she had looked forward to their sessions. "Ethan gave up on me, but you didn't."

"I thought of it as a challenge. And you needed to pass the course."

What she had needed, Hannah remembered, was him. She'd actually learned the concepts a great deal faster than she'd let on. But she'd enjoyed being tutored by him, enjoyed knowing that Jackson was coming over for a couple of hours to try to drum calculus theory into her head.

"Well I did, thanks to you." Hannah looked at him over her spoon, debating, then plunging forward. "Where did you go when you left?"

"New York."

"Wow." The large city was a completely different world from Storkville. "You really did want to get lost, didn't you?"

"I wanted to be busy," he corrected. "And I had been offered a position at one of the teaching hospitals there."

He'd never told her. "To teach?"

He laughed. Obviously she had more regard for his abilities than he'd had. "To learn. And I did. I learned a great deal."

"Well, we can certainly use all that knowledge right here in Storkville. It looks like we're going to have a fresh flock of babies here, soon. Not the least of which is my cousin Gwenyth's."

"So she's staying on?"

Hannah nodded. "She's determined. Gertie helped her find her own place. It's right next to Ben Crowe's ranch. I promised to help her move in on the weekend, not that there's going to be a lot to move in."

"Need help?"

"Always."

He inclined his head. "Count me in."

Her smile was wide, drawing him in. "I was hoping you'd say that."

He stopped sampling his dessert. "So we're officially friends again?"

"I never stopped being your friend, Jackson. Even when I thought you'd stopped being mine."

He believed her. It made grappling with his feelings that much harder.

Chapter Nine

Jackson wasn't quite sure how he had got himself roped into this. One minute, he was dropping by the daycare center as had become his habit, the next minute, he was knee-deep in strange party favors, lopsided cardboard cartoon characters, and enough red-white-and-blue crepe paper ribbon to cordon off Central Park from the rest of New York City.

Hannah, it became rapidly apparent, was in the middle of getting ready for the first birthday party to be held at the daycare center, and it was obviously going to be a major event.

It had been after hours when he'd arrived and she had pulled him into the front room immediately. He'd thought there was some sort of an emergency until he saw all the disassembled party decorations. She put him to work cutting out an endless parade of dancing elves who were, eventually, going to find their way along the walls.

Sitting at the coffee table, he paused to look at her beside him. She was cutting out a squadron of forest animals. The party boy, she'd informed him, loved animals. And Hannah always aimed to please.

Her hair kept falling into her face as she concentrated, and she kept pushing it back, only to have it fall again. An odd feeling was shimmering through him. He realized that it was contentment. "You know, I'd forgotten about this."

She spared him a quick glance, then looked back at what she was doing. She'd already nicked three fingers and didn't want to make it a complete set if she could help it. "Forgotten about what?"

He laughed. The entire area was covered with party crafts. Until half an hour ago when the last of the children had gone home with their parents, she'd had all her charges engaged in what looked like a cottage industry about to take off. They'd been excited about it, too. Because she had been.

He leaned over and pushed back the wayward strand behind her ear. "About how overboard you can get when it comes to holidays and birthdays."

"I do not go overboard," she sniffed. Then honesty had her adding, "Exactly."

"Yeah, you do," he told her fondly, finishing another nimble-footed elf. He took a second to admire his work before starting on the next one. "Don't you think this is a bit much for pre-schoolers?"

"This is exactly right for pre-schoolers. I can't wait for Halloween to come. Then I'll show you overboard."

He bet she would, too. "I repeat, don't you think it's a bit much for pre-schoolers?"

"No," she protested. "They're the ones who enjoy it most of all, who are still into the magic of it."

He raised a brow as he glanced her way. "Aren't you getting Halloween confused with Christmas?"

She laughed. To her, it was all magic because children were magic. And because each holiday was filled with the magic of warm memories. "Nope. Believe me, I get nothing confused with Christmas." She grinned impishly. "Maybe you should brace yourself."

He looked at her, wondering what she was up to. "For what?"

"For Christmas—and to be utterly overwhelmed." She went all out for Christmas, starting at the very beginning of the month and leaving all the decorations up until after New Year's. Ethan had always said that she did too much, but when he'd said it, it had sounded far more like complaining than when Jackson had said it just now.

Overwhelmed. That would be the word for it, he thought, trying not to look as if he was staring at her. "That happened the first time you ever walked into my life."

He was teasing her now, she thought. "We went to elementary school together."

"Yeah, I know." Carefully, he completed the elf's feet before going on to easier details.

She stopped cutting, mystified. "How could you possibly remember back that far?"

"I remember." Then, because he sensed she didn't believe him, he went on to prove it to her. "You had on a pink dress and a pink bow in your hair. I remember looking at you and thinking that you looked twice as sweet as cotton candy.''

Now she knew he was teasing her. "Five-year-old boys don't think like that.''

"How would you know?" He sent her a smug look. "Ever been a five-year-old boy?''

"No." That had nothing to do with it. She'd been around them enough, volunteering her time at the hospital children's ward before she'd ever had the opportunity to have her own daycare center.

"Then don't pretend to know what they're thinking. Besides," he added, "it was a harmless enough thought then.''

"Then?" she echoed. As in the difference between then and now? Hannah looked at him more closely, the cut-outs temporarily forgotten. "Does that mean it's not harmless now?''

That had been a slip. Jackson laughed at her quick uptake. "You know, for a daycare center owner, you ask questions like an interrogating district attorney. There. Done," he pronounced, retiring his scissors.

He did nice work, she thought, surveying the long chain of elves. Reaching over to the three rolls of crepe paper closest to her, she presented them to him. "Right, now the D.A. would like you to start hanging streamers." She pointed vaguely around the room, leaving it up to his imagination where to place them.

Jackson looked down at the rolls dubiously. "I hope you don't mean all over the house." He looked around. "This is one big house, Hannah.''

She grinned. "Afraid of a little work?''

"No...but this is one big house," he repeated.

"Just do the first floor and the banister, that'll be

enough. I'll do the outside of the house tomorrow morning.'' There was a sign she'd stayed up making last night that she knew would gladden Anthony's heart. The little boy had lost his mother this year and his father was really worried about his son facing the first birthday without her. Hannah was determined to do whatever she could to make it a happy occasion for the six-year-old.

''You know,'' Jackson said, twisting the three strands together awkwardly, ''this isn't exactly a major holiday.'' Two of the rolls fell from his hand, unraveling as they went.

Hannah stooped to retrieve them. Holding one, she quickly rewound the other, making her way to Jackson as she went. ''That all depends.''

''On what?'' he wanted to know.

''On whether it's your birthday or not.'' She thrust the red roll into his hands and began rewinding the white one.

''If it were my birthday, I wouldn't want any fuss.''

She raised her eyes to his. ''Yes, I remember.'' And then a smile curved her mouth. ''Now tell me if I ever listened.''

The question evoked warm memories. It had been Hannah who had always made him feel special. ''No, I can't say you ever did.'' He surveyed the room, trying to envision how she could outdo herself when Halloween came along. ''You really going to do more for Halloween?''

''You bet. I plan to start decorating in the middle of October—''

''Why, in heaven's name?'' he asked, cutting her

off. "You're not the local department store, you don't have to sell anyone on anything."

She stared at him. What did that have to do with anything? "It's not about selling, it's about festivities."

He snorted. "Halloween is about candy and getting sick on it. And doing what you shouldn't."

He had her there. "That one you're going to have to explain."

Reunited with the second runaway roll of crepe paper, he began twisting the chain again. "Think about it. All year long, you tell kids not to talk to strangers, not to take candy from people, and then one night a year, you tell them that it's okay to go out and collect as much as they can carry, blackmailing people while they're at it."

Hannah looked at him uncertainly. "Blackmailing?"

"Sure." His fingers were getting red and blue from the crepe paper. Jackson wiped them on his jeans and continued twisting the strands. "What else would you call yelling out 'trick or treat?'"

Someone had siphoned all the fun out of the Jackson she had known. "Boy, you must be a regular joy to be around when Christmas comes, Ebenezer. Tell me, what did the big city do to you?"

Living in New York had only honed his attitude. It was living in a home with no joy that had initially forged the feelings he now had. Although, for a little while, when he had interacted with Hannah and her family, that attitude had been placed on temporary hold.

"Opened my eyes up a little more," he told her.

She shook her head, taking the crepe paper rolls from him. He was creating tight curls rather than festive chains. Quickly, she began to braid the three strands together. Long chains began to fall from her fast moving fingers. "I don't know about your eyes, but it certainly sucked out your soul."

No, he thought. My soul I left behind me when I left Storkville.

Suddenly, she wanted to make him smile, to wipe away that serious look from his eyes. "Guess it's my sworn duty to get it back for you. Here." Quickly, she dipped into the candy bowl on the coffee table and peeled away the wrappings on a miniature candy bar. Then, as he began to protest, she popped it into his mouth. "Something to start the process and sweeten you up."

Jackson removed the chocolate from between his lips, holding it in his fingers. "I don't need sweetening. Guys aren't supposed to be sweet."

"Says who?" She stopped braiding and looked at the candy bar in his fingers. "Now look, it's melting in your hand. Eat it." With a small salute, he returned it to his mouth and consumed it—then froze as she playfully took hold of his wrist and proceeded to lick the melted chocolate from his two fingers. "There, now you won't get chocolate on anything."

When she raised her eyes to his, the playful expression slipped away from her face. In its place, as sudden as a twister rising from nowhere, was an urgent longing that wound all through her. What she saw in his eyes was desire. The same kind of desire she felt rattling the bars of her restraint.

"Except, maybe you," he murmured, bringing his mouth down to hers.

She could taste the chocolate. Taste, too, the wild, sharp tang of passion mixed with desire on his mouth. The chain she had been braiding so swiftly fell from her lax fingers, sinking to the floor in a partially unraveled heap. It was the furthest thing from her mind as she wound her arms around Jackson's neck, wound her thoughts completely around the man who had occupied her mind and her heart for all these years.

Jackson deepened the kiss, tightened the embrace. Did she have any idea what she did to him? Any inkling of how crazy she made him, standing there before him, all pure and tempting?

"I thought we were decorating for Anthony's birthday, not Valentine's Day," Gertie quipped as she walked in, carrying a box of more cute little stuffed forest creatures she'd unearthed in her own basement. Her children had played with them in their day. Amazingly enough, they were still in pretty good shape. She plunked the box down on the sofa beside the coffee table. "Thought you might want these." Her eyes twinkled with approval behind her glasses. "Didn't realize you were testing each other's lips for future apple-dunking contests."

Flustered, running her hand through her hair, Hannah shot her a warning look. "Gertie—"

The older woman held up her hand in front of her, as if to shield her eyes. "Sorry, the light's too bright in here for me to stay. I'll just go and see about feeding the twins."

The twins. How could she have forgotten that it was their dinnertime? Chagrined, she quickly stepped away from Jackson and crossed to the portable playpen where the twins were playing. "I should be doing that."

Following her, Gertie shook her head. She glanced over her shoulder at Jackson. "I'd say you had your hands pretty full, Hannah. Not that I can blame you."

If her cheeks got any redder, she was going to spontaneously combust, Hannah thought ruefully. "That's all right, Gertie. Why don't you see about helping out with the birthday decorations instead? I like feeding the babies."

"She has a weakness for strained carrots in her hair," Gertie confided to Jackson.

Taking an interest, and welcoming the chance to change the topic and make a quick getaway from the decorations, he joined Hannah at the playpen. He looked down at the twins. Today, he hadn't even bothered going through the charade of examining them. The twins were healthy and doing well.

"They're not eating well?"

"They're eating," Hannah replied, bending over to pick up Sammy. The little boy smiled gleefully as she took him into her arms. "Like typical babies. Half goes into their stomachs, half they wear. It's a trade-off."

Jackson pretended to look skeptical. "As their doctor, I should take part in their feeding at least once, make sure that they're getting their proper nutrition."

She welcomed his company. Too much, she knew, but she'd deal with that at another time. Right now, she just wanted to enjoy having Jackson near her.

There was no denying how much she cared about him. Words hadn't passed between them about that, at least not about how she felt about him at the present moment. She'd only confessed to having had a crush on him in the past. They probably never would talk about the present, which was fine with her. It was far less embarrassing that way.

But that didn't alter the facts any. And the fact was that she loved him. And always would.

If Jackson wasn't sleepwalking through his life, he'd realize that, she thought. But it was better this way, because if they talked about it, if one of them said the words out loud, then Jackson might feel compelled to tell her something noble, like he was very flattered, but—

That awful word: *but*. Positive that he would use it, Hannah wasn't sure if she was up to hearing it. What she couldn't cope with was better left alone.

Turning, she handed Sammy to him then picked up Steffie. "Okay, just remember you asked for this," she warned.

Yes, he thought, following her into the kitchen, he had.

"So, what's on the menu tonight?" he asked, looking around.

There were two high chairs at the table where two chairs had once been. The latter were now standing against the far wall, two retired sentries still at attention, still waiting to be pressed into duty. The table, like the house, was from another era and looked out of place beside the high chairs—and the profusion of decorations that seemed to be everywhere in the room.

Jackson's eyes widened as he turned to look at Hannah. "My God, you've struck here, too."

"Strained lamb stew and yes, I did," Hannah replied, answering both his question and his statement as she slid Steffie into her high chair and snapped the belt around her middle, securing her in place. Jackson echoed her movements with Sammy. "Anthony might walk in here. I just wanted to make sure that the whole house looked festive to him. It's the least I can do."

"Least?" he echoed.

"Because he's facing this without his mother for the first time. His father told me she always used to make a fuss." She gave a small half shrug, awkward with having to explain herself. "I just want him to be happy."

She really was something else, he thought. "You want the whole world to be happy."

Her eyes met his. "Nothing wrong with that."

"No," he agreed. "Nothing wrong with that." It was just impossible, that was all, he added silently.

She moved to the stove to check on the two jars that Gertie had left warming. "I just wish I had a little more time to clean the place up properly, but I've been so busy. Do you realize that I haven't even made a dent in the attic?"

To him, attics were for storing, not for cleaning. "Why don't you just leave the door closed and forget about it?"

She looked at him over her shoulder. "Forget about it? I'm looking forward to it. There're some old trunks up there I haven't had a chance to open up yet. I'm saving that for a special treat."

"Treat?" Jackson didn't think of rifling through old, musty trunks as something to look forward to.

"Sure, they're probably full of old memories." Turning the burner off, she gingerly removed the jars then tested the contents of both by spooning a drop from each onto the inside of her wrist. Satisfied with the temperature, she brought the jars over to the table. "Maybe Aunt Jane even kept diaries."

Jackson took the spoon Hannah handed him and picked up one of the jars from the table. "Isn't that an invasion of privacy?"

"Only if my great-aunt were alive. Now that she's gone, it's just like sharing the important parts of her life with her."

The workings of her mind left him in bemused awe. Coaxing the spoon between Sammy's lips, Jackson could only shake his head. "Like I said, you should have been a lawyer. You're completely wasted as a daycare center owner."

Steffie's appetite was in rare form tonight, she noted. Hannah could hardly get the spoon to the baby fast enough. "Oh, I don't know. I find working with the children pretty fulfilling. As well as exhausting."

He smiled as Sammy finally opened his mouth wider. "You do seem to have a flair for it. Praise for you is running pretty high."

"Oh?" She looked at him. What had he heard? "Whose?"

"The mothers of some of the children in your center." More than a few had gone out of their way to tell him how much happier their children seemed to be now that they were attending the daycare center. "They can't say enough about you."

Hannah beamed. It was nice hearing that her efforts were appreciated. "Really?"

"Really." He glanced in her direction, seeing her smile. "You had to know you were doing a good job."

"Well, yes, I knew," she admitted. "But it's nice to know that it's appreciated. And that what I'm doing is making a difference in someone's life."

That, he would have thought, went without saying. The Hannah he knew was bright enough to intuit that. "Just knowing that they can leave their children in the care of someone who they trust, who they know is responsible and loving lifts a great weight off their shoulders."

Using the bib she'd tied on Steffie, she cleaned the little girl's very messy chin. "That's me, the weight lifter." He laughed and she looked at him. "What?"

"Nothing, I just thought that might be a good costume."

"Costume?" She was immediately interested. "For what?"

Jackson saw the alert look in her eyes and, too late, realized his mistake. "Never mind."

"Tell me," she prodded. "I won't make you put up any more streamers."

"You always did have a flair for bribery." She'd probably hear about it anyway, he reasoned. "The hospital's throwing a costume party next week to welcome the new director to the staff."

"Costume party? What are you going as?"

The whole thing was pure foolishness and he didn't have time for it. "The invisible man."

Her eyes narrowed. "You're not going."

Jackson inclined his head. "Good guess."

"But you have to go," she insisted. "You don't want to insult the new director, do you?"

Jackson didn't particularly care about the director one way or another as long as the man didn't interfere with his relationship with his patients. "What I don't want is to feel like an idiot."

She grinned. "You won't. Just leave everything to me."

Jackson sighed. "Oh, all right."

That, he realized later, was his first mistake.

Chapter Ten

"Aren't pirates supposed to have a wooden leg, a patch over one eye and a parrot on their shoulder?"

Feeling decidedly uncomfortable, Jackson walked out of the guest room where he'd gone to put on the costume that Hannah had got for him for the party. He was on the verge of phoning in his apologies, or simply taking his chances being branded a no-show. It wasn't as if his career depended on attending.

Anything seemed better than walking around outside like this.

And then he saw her, and his thoughts about attending began to change radically. He hadn't realized that while he was struggling with his sense of values and putting on his costume, she'd be putting on hers.

Jackson contracted a severe case of dry mouth as he surveyed the way her blouse dipped low with every breath she exhaled. Walking over hot coals would be worth seeing her like this.

He looked nothing short of fantastic. She'd known he would the moment she'd seen the pirate's costume in the shop. The part suited him far better than that of a knight in shining armor, the costume she'd been considering until she saw this one. There was something very roguish about Jackson that this brought out in spades.

"Not my pirates." Tucking her tambourine under her arm, Hannah adjusted the sword at his hip. "My pirates have twenty-twenty vision in their mesmerizing blue eyes and two feet, not one. And as for the parrot, it would definitely interfere when they stopped to kiss the woman they rescued from another pirate king's ship." She grinned mischievously, adding, "A pirate king who had a patch over his eye, a wooden leg and a parrot."

He laughed shortly, looking himself over critically in the mirror that hung above the carved table in the hall. He supposed he didn't look like a complete fool—and if nothing else, his going to this function did seem to make Hannah happy.

"Sounds more like a Hollywood version than something out of Robert Louis Stevenson."

Hannah shrugged nonchalantly. She was trying very hard not to stare, but his pirate's shirt was open almost to his waist, and the view from where she stood was disarming, to put it mildly. "You have your fantasies, I'll have mine."

He looked at her standing beside him in the mirror. "Is that what this is?" Jackson turned toward her, a warm smile on his lips. "A fantasy of yours? To be attending a hospital function with a man wearing wide pants, high-heeled boots and a shirt with sleeves big enough to hide three or four of his patients in?''

"Sure," she answered glibly, turning her face up to his, "what's yours?"

His eyes washed over her. With her wrists and neck laden down with thin golden chains, her chestnut hair swirling about her like a wayward autumn breeze, Hannah looked every inch the gypsy. He could almost hear her reading fortunes. He knew what he'd like his to be.

"To be attending a hospital function with a woman dressed in a swirling red skirt and a gaily colored scarf jauntily tied at her waist."

In reply, Hannah raised the tambourine she was holding and hit it rhythmically with the heel of her hand. She shook it so that the tiny cymbals all along its perimeter chimed in. "Then I'm happy to be able to fulfill your wish."

If only, he thought.

Dragging himself out of his mental revelry, Jackson looked down at the costume and wondered if the sword was going to trip him up during the evening. Or if he'd wind up hitting someone with the scabbard. "My real wish is to get out of these clothes."

Her grin widened as her eyes began to sparkle with humor. "Careful, doctor, you have a reputation to maintain."

When she looked at him like that, he nearly swallowed his tongue. Pretending to be oblivious was next to impossible so he didn't even try. "Just when did you get this damn sexy?"

Hannah shrugged, sending her peasant blouse slipping seductively off her shoulder. As she moved it back into place, the look in his eyes registered, pleasing her beyond words. The compliment he'd just paid her, after the years of self doubts she'd endured, did her far more good than he could ever begin to guess.

Her laugh was low and seductive as she went to get the long fringed shawl that she'd chosen to go with the costume. "Maybe it's the full moon that brings it out of me."

Opening the front door, Jackson pointed toward the sky. "That's a crescent moon."

"So it is." Undaunted, Hannah laughed. "You should see me when it gets full."

He resisted the urge to kiss her, knowing that if he gave in, they might never make it through the front door. Certainly not to the party. "You're really something else, you know that?"

He was stalling. She placed both hands to his back and pushed him through the doorway. "And you are going to make us late if we stand here talking any longer."

So much for the best laid plans of mice and men, he thought with an inward sigh. "You know, I really don't want to go."

What she knew was that this function was important and that there were certain rules of protocol to follow, even for a former rebel like Jackson Caldwell. She figured that since he'd told her about the invitation, that meant that deep down at least part of him wanted her to talk him into going. Hannah had never shirked a duty, and she wasn't about to begin now with Jackson.

Calling out a final good night to Gertie, who'd volunteered to remain with Gwenyth to baby-sit and was upstairs bathing the twins, Hannah slipped her arm through Jackson's. "You really don't want to offend the new director right off the bat, do you? Besides, it'll be fun."

Jackson frowned. "Not my definition of fun."

But, oddly enough, it was.

On the whole, he'd never really cared for any kind of formal parties. He'd seen far too many of them in his parents' house. People milling around, pretending to have fun while making empty conversation as they held cocktail glasses they were constantly refilling. People who came with one person while trying to arrange a tryst with another. He preferred dealing with people on a one-to-one basis. If it were up to him, parties in general would have been outlawed. And the first on the list would have been costume parties.

And yet, he was having a good time, almost against his will.

There was just something about experiencing the evening through Hannah's eyes that consequently, no matter how much he resisted it at first, made him enjoy himself.

In a way, it was as if he was truly seeing her for the first time. People seemed to gravitate toward her because she shone so brightly. She took an avid interest in everything and everyone. Being near her just naturally seemed to make everything better. His mood included.

He watched as she danced with the new director and Jackson suddenly found himself growing jealous of a balding, fifty-seven-year-old, out-of-shape man in a Robin Hood costume because Hannah was laughing at something he had just said to her.

If anyone had been privy to his mind, they would have said he was in love, Jackson mused. He had to do something about that.

But not tonight.

"You certainly know how to work a room," he murmured to Hannah as he came up next to her. The director's attention had been temporarily commandeered by the head nurse dressed as a duchess. The woman whisked the breathless Robin Hood away. Jackson handed Hannah a cup of punch.

She took the cup in both hands and held it first before sipping. "What do you mean?"

"Everywhere I turn, I hear people mentioning your name." He nodded at the man who had just relinquished her. "The director thinks you'd be wonderful at fund-raising. He's about this far," Jackson held his thumb and forefinger a half-inch apart, "from offering you a position with the hospital."

That was flattering, but she shook her head. "Not interested."

Jackson played devil's advocate. "You never know. The offer might come with a lucrative benefits package, not to mention a tempting salary."

"I don't need a lucrative benefits package, I'm young and alone," she pointed out, trying not to dwell on the deep holes those words dug within her, "and there are far more important things in life than a salary, tempting or otherwise." She heard Jackson laugh as she brought the cup to her lips. "What?"

Her answer had pleased him a great deal. "You would have been a revelation to my father. He felt that there was nothing more important than money.'' His mouth hardened as he thought of the countless affairs that had littered his father's life—and stained his mother's. Jackson looked off into space. ''Not even momentary lapses into recreational fields.''

Lost, Hannah tugged on his sleeve until he looked at her again. ''How's that again?''

''Nothing,'' he said, waving his thoughts away. This was no time to be talking about his father. ''So, that's it?'' He studied her face, looking for some indication whether she was serious or strictly making conversation. ''You're going to be running a daycare center for the rest of your life?''

She finished her punch, but continued to hold the cup in her hands. Maybe it was the punch that made her hear it, but she didn't like his implication. ''You make it sound insignificant.''

He hadn't meant to offend her, he'd just thought that her goals were loftier. ''Not insignificant, just not, well, big,'' he said for lack of a better word.

Cocking her head, she looked at him, the empty cup dangling from her fingertips. ''Influencing children's lives, giving them a warm, solid base, that isn't big to you?''

It looked as if he was treading on sacred territory. Jackson backtracked. ''I didn't mean that.''

''I should hope not.'' She managed to say it before the smile slipped out, betraying her. Jackson knew he was off the hook.

Because the strongest thing Hannah ever drank was an occasional glass of very weak wine, the punch was having more of an effect on her than it should have. Too late she discovered that the fruity taste that had tantalized her tongue was not all due to fruit obtained in the produce section of her local grocery store. A warm glow lit in her stomach in response to the look Jackson was giving her.

Her eyes teased his. "Dance with me, Jackson." She lifted her hands to his, waiting. "Make me feel as pretty as you made me sound earlier tonight."

He gladly took her into his arms. Holding her here, in front of all these people, was safe. He couldn't do anything that might lead to something else, not here. And if holding her close to him like this constituted sweet agony, so be it. At least he was holding her.

"You don't need a press agent for that, Hannah. You are pretty." And then, mid-sentence, he changed his mind. "No, I take it back. You're not pretty."

The tune coming from the orchestra comprised predominantly of high-school seniors in music class barely registered. "I'm not?"

"No, you're not. Wild flowers are pretty." He leaned his face into hers, whispering against her ear. "Roses are beautiful. And you, Hannah Dawson Brady, are definitely a rose."

She could feel her eyes stinging. No one had ever said anything that lovely to her before. Not even Ethan when he was trying to flatter her. "Now you're going to make me cry."

She wasn't kidding, he realized. He wished he had a handkerchief, but his costume hadn't come with pockets. "Don't do that. I'll have fourteen people in the immediate vicinity pummel me to the ground if they see you crying while you're dancing with me."

The entreaty had done the trick, lightening the mood. She laughed. "You say the silliest things."

He smiled into her eyes. "Must be the company I keep." Jackson pressed his cheek against her hair, for a moment just steeping himself in the scent and feel of her. He felt his senses becoming intoxicated. "What's that you're wearing?"

Nestled within the warmth of his embrace, she felt as if she was dancing in a dream. "Clothes."

He almost laughed and without thinking, kissed her hair. "No, I mean what's that scent?"

Ripples of pleasure undulated through her. She could feel his breath on her skin. "Punch?"

She could taste it, feel it, every time she exhaled. Or was that simply her being intoxicated by him? She wasn't sure, but she was more than willing to carry out experiments to find out.

She was slightly tipsy, he thought, and all the more adorable for it. "No, I mean the perfume you're wearing. What is it?"

She thought for a second, taking mental inventory. "Maybe that's the herbal shampoo," she guessed, looking up at him. "I'm not wearing any perfume."

And maybe, he thought, it was just the essence of her that filled his senses. Maybe it was just the smell of her skin, of her hair, of her, that was making him crazy.

He held her closer as they danced.

The trip back to her house seemed to end before it had begun. Hannah had no sooner sat back, leaning against the headrest, her eyes slipping closed, than she was opening them again. It was time to get out of the car.

She tried not to be too obvious as she stretched,

getting the kinks out of her shoulders. She turned to Jackson. "Now, aren't you glad I made you go?"

He pretended to hold on to the lie, knowing she knew better. "No."

"Your nose is growing." She touched it as she made the announcement, leaning over the emergency brake, causing emergencies of her own in his blood as he looked at her and her receding blouse.

This had to be some kind of a celestial test he decided, and if he wasn't careful, he was going to be flunking. Big time.

"Okay." Getting out, he rounded the hood and opened her door for her. "I'm glad you made me go." Still, he wanted her clear on why he was glad he'd gone. "But it was only a good time because you were there."

"Good." Taking his hand, she allowed him to help her out. "Perfect thing to say." She rose to her feet, then remained where she stood for a second. "Especially to a woman who's having trouble feeling her legs."

"Did we dance too much?" he asked.

She shook her head. "No, you can never dance too much. But on the subject of too much, I think maybe I did have too much punch."

Surprised, he looked at her incredulously. Up until now, he'd assumed she was just tired. "Two glasses over the course of an entire evening is hardly too much to drink."

She pointed toward the front porch and the legion of steps that had formed in her absence. "Then why did the stairs suddenly get steeper and taller?"

He looked at them and then laughed, playing along.

"Maybe it's the lighting." Then, in the spirit of the evening and the costume he was wearing, he went with an impulse. "But I tell you what, there's a perfectly simple solution to this navigation problem you seem to think you have."

"Oh?" She raised her eyes to look at him, trying to keep the buzzing in her head at a minimum. "What?"

"This."

The next moment, Hannah found herself being scooped up in his arms. A thrill ricocheted through her before she thought to protest. "Wait, you'll hurt your back."

He mustered a wounded look. "Are you trying to insult my manhood?"

"Never," she breathed. Settling in, she twined her arms around his neck and sighed in contentment as he carried her up the porch steps.

"Good, because a ten-year-old, out-of-shape weakling could carry you up the stairs, Hannah. I've got paperweights that weigh more than you do."

"You must have a lot of paper on your desk," she murmured, her breath warm against his chest as she rested her head there.

She closed her eyes, absorbing the sweet sensation of feeling him carry her up the stairs to her front door. Of the rhythmic beating of his heart. With a sigh, she waited for him to set her down.

When he didn't she opened her eyes to look at him. "What?"

He wanted to go on holding her just a little longer. "Just thinking."

He sounded so serious. "What?"

If he told her, the moment would end. Maybe she'd even be annoyed with him. He wouldn't blame her if she were. "Thoughts I shouldn't be."

"Maybe you shouldn't be thinking them," she told him quietly as he set her down and her feet touched the porch. Feeling oddly confident, she took out her key. "Maybe you should be doing something about them instead."

The key that he took from her nearly slipped through his fingers as he heard her say words he fervently wished he could obey. Jackson turned his back to her as he unlocked her door.

"You don't know what you're saying, Hannah." Unlocking the door, he stood back to let her enter first.

"I think I do." She walked into the foyer. There was only one lone lamp on, casting a dim pool of light on the Oriental rug. Her heart began to pound. "I haven't had that much punch, if that's what you're thinking."

When she looked at him like that, he felt himself sinking into her eyes. "What I'm thinking is that I want you, Hannah. And I shouldn't."

"Why?" The word hung in the air between them as she turned her face up to his. "Is wanting me such a terrible thing?"

"Yes." He was losing, damn it. Losing the struggle with honor, with decency. "No."

She swallowed, silently willing him to make love with her. To take her now and put an end to the ache in her soul. "Which is it?"

"Depends on who you are," he told her softly, his fingers tangling in her hair. "Me. Or you."

"I'm me," she told him, her voice hardly above an inviting whisper. "And for me, having you want me isn't a terrible thing." She drew the only conclusion she could. And prayed he'd tell her that she was wrong. "That means it must be a terrible thing for you."

"Hannah, this isn't a game."

She'd never believed that, not for a moment. The stakes were far too high for it to be a game to her. Her eyes searched his face for a clue as to what he was thinking. "But there will be winners and losers, won't there?"

"Yes." Jackson framed her face, wanting her more than he wanted to wake up the next morning. "There will be winners and losers. And I don't want you to be a loser."

She wouldn't be, not if he made love with her. Not if she could, just once, feel that he was hers. She had been his for so very long.

"Put your money where your mouth is," she coaxed, her lips a fraction away from his.

He surrendered. "I'd rather put my mouth where your mouth is."

"That, too," she whispered.

Rising up on her toes, Hannah ended the internal debate for him by sealing her mouth to his.

The instant she did, Jackson pulled her urgently into his arms, unleashing the wild, erotic emotions that had been beating their wings so wildly within him.

More than anything in the world, he wanted to make love with her. To take her and make her his once and for all, the way he already had a hundred, no, a thousand times in his mind. Since before the days when Ethan had had any claim to her. Since before the days when he knew he couldn't taint her this way.

But tonight, there was something about her, about the uninhibited look in her eyes. Something about the feel of her body as she'd held it against his while they were dancing.

Something about her.

Jackson was helpless to fight off the urgent demands of his own body when faced with the warm, open invitation of hers.

Standing in the darkened foyer, he felt himself getting lost in the taste of her mouth, the sweetness of her breath, the softness of her body as it molded itself to his.

He kissed her over and over again, his blood rushing, his mind swimming. Caressing the curves and swells that had so sorely tempted him all this time, he fought to keep from pulling her costume away from her. He wanted tonight to be memorable for her, not something to be filed away as a result of unchecked passion that had gotten out of hand. Above all, he wanted to pleasure her.

The sound of crying pierced the disjointed thoughts racing through his mind.

Gasping for air, Hannah drew her head back. How could she have forgotten? "The twins."

They weren't alone. The entreaties that were battering their souls and their bodies echoed off into the night, fading.

Chapter Eleven

The realization of what she had almost let herself do penetrated. She had completely forgotten herself. Completely forgotten her obligations and had been a heartbeat away from giving in to needs that had been her daily companion for as long as she could remember—longer—at the expense of two small babies who were helpless without her.

"I'd—I'd better tell Gertie she's free to go," Hannah stammered.

"Speaking of going, I guess I should be doing the same," Jackson murmured.

Why was it, when he was with this woman, he forgot everything he had ever promised himself to abide by? Why did he constantly put himself into situations with her that made him yearn to turn his back on everything he knew he couldn't in good conscience forsake?

Unable to answer his own questions, Jackson began to cross to the door.

It shouldn't end like this, on such an awkward note. She didn't want him to think she was rejecting him or what had almost happened between them. What she was rejecting was the timing. Her hand on the banister, she paused. "Can I interest you in a cup of coffee?"

She could interest him in a great many things, coffee only being at the end of the long list, he thought. He shook his head. Jackson had to admit, at least to himself, that he was in far deeper than he'd ever imagined he would be. Resisting Hannah was becoming increasingly more difficult each time he was faced with the temptation.

This time the babies had come to his rescue, so to speak. The next time, there might not be a wake-up call coming to the aid of his lax conscience at the eleventh hour. The next time, he might give in and make love with Hannah.

And become hopelessly caught in a tender, tempting trap he had absolutely no business being in.

Jackson sighed inwardly. Once he was with Hannah, it seemed almost impossible to do the right thing. Heaven knew, it was almost humanly impossible to keep her at arms' length.

Maybe then, a small voice within him whispered, you shouldn't be around Hannah.

"Coffee sounds great, but it'll only keep me awake and it's getting late," he said opening the door. "And I've got to be at the hospital early tomorrow morning."

It was a lie, but it was the best he could do with

his brain scrambled this way. He wasn't accustomed to lying, especially not to her.

Hannah looked at him in silence. He was lying. She could feel it even if she couldn't understand why. Was she that unappealing to him? Why did he always stop himself at the last moment, as if he were suddenly thinking better of what he was about to do? As if he realized that he'd almost done something stupid?

The thought hurt and she put it out of her mind. But the feeling lingered. She hadn't been woman enough for Ethan to keep him from looking elsewhere for company and sensual pleasure. Was the same true with Jackson? Didn't he find her attractive enough at least to try to make her change her mind? To try to get her to go to bed with him? If one of the babies hadn't cried, if Gertie hadn't been here, would she have wound up being embarrassed anyway, not by what she'd wanted to do, but by what Jackson didn't want to do?

"Wouldn't want to interfere with your hours," she agreed woodenly. She suddenly realized that he was still wearing the pirate costume she'd rented for him. "Um, you can bring the costume back tomorrow if you like—or whenever you want to stop by," she added, afraid that he might think she was taking his presence in her life for granted.

Because she was.

Not for granted, never for granted, but she'd come to expect it and look forward to it the way someone looked forward to being in the presence of a secret treasure that came into their lives every so often.

Jackson looked down at himself, chagrined at the oversight. How the hell could a man forget he was wearing a billowing shirt and wide trousers? Unless, he thought, that man had just kissed Hannah.

There was no sense in going home like this, not when his clothes were here. Shrugging out of the shirt, he began walking toward the guest room where he'd left his clothes. "No, I might as well get this over with now. I'll just go into the other bedroom and take the rest of this off—"

The sharp intake of breath had them both looking up the stairs to the source. Their eyes locked with Gertie's. Even at this distance, it was easy to see that Gertie's were filled with amused, unabashed pleasure.

She waved them both back to what she presumed they were about to do. "Sorry, didn't mean to walk in on anything."

It didn't take a clairvoyant to know what Gertie was thinking. "You didn't," Hannah told her quickly, eager to clear up the misunderstanding before it got out of hand. "It's not what you're thinking."

"Thinking?" Gertie covered her bosom with clasped hands, the soul of innocence. "Why I'm not thinking anything except that I can take the twins over to my place. Ask Gwenyth to come along, too." The gleam in her eye, so guileless a second ago, turned positively wicked. "Give you and Jackson time to really play doctor and patient."

"Gertie!" Almost speechless, her throat drier than the summer desert at noon, Hannah could only manage to squeak her protest.

Gertie looked at her impatiently. "Well, if I said 'make love together,' you'd get all flustered and pink." She gestured at Hannah's face. "Just the way you are right now. Honestly, Hannah, you really are old enough to be doing this, you know.'' She looked meaningfully at Jackson, who, for his part, was torn between being amused and feeling sympathetic for what Hannah was going through.

''We're not *doing* anything,'' Hannah insisted. ''Jackson's only taking off the costume so he can give it to me to take back to the rental shop tomorrow, along with mine.''

A quick look at both their faces confirmed the explanation. Gertie shook her head in disappointment as she came down the stairs. ''I just don't know what this new generation is coming to. If everyone were like you two, the town council'd have to change the name of this town again, this time to Dullsville.''

Tired, upset and at a loss as to how to cope with all the emotions that had been let loose to run rampant through her, Hannah just kissed her soft cheek as Gertie came to the bottom of the stairs. ''Thank you for watching the twins, but I could really do without the running commentary.''

''No,'' Gertie pronounced astutely, looking at Hannah sternly before turning her condemning gaze on Jackson, ''you can't.''

The woman never saw him coming.

So preoccupied with her own thoughts, her own concerns, she never saw the man coming at her until it was too late. One minute she was making her way to the bed and breakfast inn just on the other side of the narrow street, the next minute he was coming at her.

A scream echoed in her throat as he plowed right into her, knocking her down.

He had no face.

Something black was wrapped around it, obscuring it from her vision. She thought she saw two dark eyes boring into her, but she couldn't be sure. It might have just been the sudden flare of panic burning into her.

And then the growing pain in her head blotted out everything before that, too, faded away.

"Can you hear me?" a voice asked.

She felt someone patting her hand and she struggled to open her eyes. When she did, she found herself looking up into the face of a woman she had never seen before. An older woman with short gray hair and a kindly, concerned smile that widened now with relief. The woman's eyes, bright and alert, seemed to be searching her face for something.

"Are you all right, my dear?"

Holding tightly to the woman's hand, she raised herself up. The immediate world refused to come into focus, spinning around her.

"I don't know," she answered hoarsely. Fear and confusion fought a duel with tiny, pointy straight pins, jabbing at her as she tried to pull her thoughts together.

And found that there were none to pull.

Panic superseded pain.

Eyes widening, she stared at the woman. Her voice shook when she asked, "Where am I?"

"This is Storkville, dear," the woman told her kindly. "And some horrible creature just bashed you over the head with some object he was holding and stole your purse and the overnight satchel you were carrying. I saw the whole thing," she volunteered, then added with a note of frustration, "but I couldn't stop him." She shook her head. "I don't even know who he was, he was wearing some kind of a stocking over his head like in those movies about bank robbers." The older woman shook her head again, lamenting. "Nothing like this has ever happened in Storkville before."

"Storkville?" she echoed, trying to sneak words past the excruciating pain in her head.

The name meant nothing to her. The details the other woman had just recited meant nothing to her. She didn't remember anyone hitting her, anyone taking something from her.

She couldn't remember anything.

"Yes, Storkville," the other woman repeated patiently. "Storkville, Nebraska, the most fertile city in the union, per capita, bar none." So saying, she beamed for a moment, then the smile faded as she bent closer to look her over. "I don't live far from here, dear. I was just out for my evening walk," she explained. "Why don't I take you home, make you a nice cup of hot tea? Unless you have a reservation at the bed and breakfast over there." She nodded vaguely over her shoulder at the street just beyond.

"No, I don't have a reservation," she answered hoarsely. At least, she didn't think she had one. She didn't know.

"Do you think you can walk, Emma?"

She looked up sharply at the woman. Did they know one another? Was the woman someone to her? "Why did you call me that?"

Looking perplexed, the woman touched something

at the base of her throat. A moment later, the sensation registered. Metal. She was wearing a gold chain necklace with a small oval medallion in the center.

"That's what it says engraved right there. 'Emma,'" the older woman read, then raised her eyes to her face. "That's your name, isn't it?"

The young woman looked at her blankly. "I don't know."

"I do declare, I haven't seen such a spate of excitement in this town since—can't remember when." Bustling into Jackson's office, Gertie commandeered the chair closest to his desk and settled in. "Thanks for seeing me, I brought you these." She took a small bag of cookies out of her purse and placed them on his desk. "Still a little warm," she said proudly. "I know how much you like them."

Jackson felt himself about to be steamrolled. This was the first time he'd seen Gertie since the night of the costume party when he and Hannah had almost made love. He'd made his decision on the way home that night. He'd been coming over too much, that had to stop for both their sakes.

No one could have been more surprised at Gertie's sudden appearance in his waiting room, requesting a private moment. He wondered if it had to do with Hannah.

He looked at the bag. "You really shouldn't have gone to the trouble."

"No trouble at all. I like baking. Like knowing what's going on, too," she added craftily. "Which is why I'd hate to be Tucker right now. That young man's still got his hands full, trying to find the twins' rightful parents and now he's got to deal with a mugger, too.'' Not standing on ceremony, she reached over and opened the bag she'd brought, taking out a cookie for herself. ''And I wasn't much help to him.''

He'd heard all about that. It was hard living in Storkville and not hearing local gossip making the rounds. The day after the mugging had happened, it had been the topic of conversation both in his office and at the hospital where the young woman had been brought. The poor woman had been diagnosed with temporary amnesia that, so far, gave no indication of fading.

''You gave him a description,'' Jackson pointed out.

Gertie snorted. ''Some description. A medium-sized, average-looking man with a nylon stocking on his head. If the streetlight hadn't hit that belt buckle of his with the deer head on it, there would have been nothing to set him apart from scores of other men.''

Jackson took a bite of one of Gertie's offerings and felt himself softening to the invasion. ''Not too many men running around out there with stockings pulled over their faces,'' he quipped. And then he leaned back in his chair and studied Gertie's face. ''But you didn't come just to talk to me about this mysterious woman. What's the real reason you came here, Gertie?''

Gertie purposely avoided his eyes. ''I wanted to ask your advice about my granddaughter.''

He was aware that she had several grandchildren. ''How old is she?''

Gertie waved her hand vaguely in the air. ''Young.'' And then she looked at him, leaning closer over the desk. "It's about her heart, Jackson." She took a deep breath. "It's in pain."

He paused, trying to remember the name of the pediatric cardiologist who was on staff at the hospital. "Dr. Campbell's the cardiac specialist, maybe you should be talking about this to him."

Gertie frowned. "It's not that kind of pain."

For a talkative woman, Gertie certainly did take a long time in getting to the point, Jackson thought. "Oh?"

Proceeding cautiously, Gertie nodded. "She's in love with someone."

If that was the case, he had no idea why Gertie was bringing this to his attention or what she thought he could do about it. "She told you?"

Gertie shrugged vaguely. "Some things, you just know. Anyway, she's in love with this really wonderful guy, but for some reason, they just can't seem to get together." She looked at him pointedly. "I don't think he's getting the message."

Obviously they weren't talking about adolescents. In which case this really was none of his business. "Maybe he doesn't have feelings for her."

"Oh, he has feelings," Gertie assured him firmly. "I know he has feelings. But the fact of the matter is, he didn't have the greatest relationship with his own family. Certainly not with his father and I don't think he thinks he knows how to have a relationship with a woman. Meanwhile, she—my granddaughter—" Gertie emphasized "—is just pining away in silence." Her eyes pinned him. "What can I do to help them?"

Okay, so this was about him. It had taken Jackson

a minute there, probably because he was dumb-founded that Gertie had taken it upon herself to act like some kind of go-between. He sincerely doubted that Hannah had put her up to this. Hannah would probably be mortified if she knew.

"Nothing," he told her firmly, returning her look. "There is nothing you can do. You might not have all the facts at your disposal."

She knew a runaway when she saw one. And Jackson, for whatever reason, was running from what could, no, what was, she amended, the best part of his life. "Oh, I think I do."

"No," he countered, his eyes holding hers, "you don't."

She continued with the charade though she knew that they were now both aware she wasn't talking about her granddaughter, but Hannah. "I know his father was no good, but that doesn't mean anything. Trouble is, he seems to think it does. There's no other reason for him to be holding back."

That she was right on target astounded him. But the subject was painful and he didn't want to talk about it. Jackson was perfectly aware that what his father had been was not a secret in Storkville, but that still didn't make the memory any easier to deal with.

With a terse movement, he closed the bag of cookies, silently turning down the offering. "Could be he's right."

Gertie frowned. "If that were the case, then every child of every criminal would be a criminal. You don't believe that, do you?"

She was twisting things. "That's different."

"Only if you make yourself believe that." Gertie

shook her head. "I'm not talking about my grand-daughter."

Jackson laughed shortly. "I didn't think so."

"Hannah's in love with you." Gertie knew Hannah would be furious with her if Hannah knew she was here, talking to Jackson like this, but it had to be done. Someone had to take the initiative and it looked as if neither one of them was going to do it. "She's never said a word, but I can tell." Gertie leveled her gaze at him. "And you're in love with her."

His patience wearing thin, Jackson rose from his seat. He'd heard enough. "Gertie, I don't have time to argue about this or tell you how wrong you are, I've got a patient coming in in a few minutes."

"You can argue all you want, still doesn't change anything. About either one of you," Gertie said. "Ever read the poem Evangeline?"

"No," he replied.

"Well, I did. Had to," she added matter-of-factly. "Teacher forced us. Anyway, it was set a long time ago." She could see his growing impatience, so she stepped up her pace. "When doesn't matter. The point is, there were these two young people in it. Crazy about each other. They were just about to get married when suddenly, through no fault of their own, they were separated. The rest of their lives, they kept looking for each other and missing one another over and over again. Sometimes they were only a few feet apart, but they didn't look in the right direction. Reading that poem, I wanted to scream at them, saying, 'Look, you idiot, before it's too late. She's standing right over there.'" Gertie shrugged. "'Course I couldn't then, but I can now." She rose majestically from her seat as she looked Jackson squarely in the eye, "Look, you idiot, before it's too late. She's standing right over there." Then, her head held high, Gertie crossed to the door. "All right, I've said my piece. The next step is up to you. It'd better be the right one, doctor-boy."

And with that, she swept out of the office, leaving him staring at the vacant doorway.

Jackson scrubbed his hand over his face. It was worse than he thought, and he was going to have to do something about it.

Chapter Twelve

She'd tried to be patient, she really had. Once she'd heard the rumor that he was leaving, Hannah had gone through an entire gamut of feelings: surprise, anger, numbness, and then endured them in reverse order. All without hearing a word from Jackson to either confirm or deny, or even to say hello.

The silence made her edgy. By the end of the day, Hannah figured she'd lasted as long as she could. Asking Gertie to stay with the twins and usher off the last of the parents, Hannah had driven over to Jackson's office in the small single-story complex that stood across the street from Storkville General Hospital.

Sailing into the outer office, she passed Jackson's last patient, barely nodded at the woman holding on to the little girl's hand. She hadn't come to exchange pleasantries.

Karen, Jackson's nurse, looked surprised to see her,

even more surprised that she had come without either twin. "Is he in his office, Karen?"

"Yes."

"Alone?"

Karen looked confused and slightly concerned. "Yes, but—"

That was all she needed. "Good." Hannah shot past her and walked into Jackson's office.

Busy writing up the chart of the child he had just examined and diagnosed, Jackson didn't look up immediately. He assumed it was Karen, coming to say good night before she left for the day.

His assumption faded when he heard Hannah's voice. "Is it true?"

Jackson looked up. Surprise melted. Something had told him she would come. Still, he pretended not to know what she was talking about, buying himself a little time that wouldn't matter in the long run. "Hannah, what are you doing here?"

"Is it true?" she repeated, struggling to keep the fury she felt from shaking her voice. "Are you leaving Storkville?

Giving up at least a piece of the charade, Jackson laid his pen down. "Yes, as soon as I can find a replacement." He hadn't wanted her to know, not until everything was finalized. He didn't want her to look at him with those eyes of hers and turn his selfless plans to dust. "How did you find out?"

For less than two cents, she would have punched his lights out for hurting her so.

"Rebecca mentioned to Gertie she'd heard a rumor that you were leaving and Gertie told me." Her temper began to slip out of the reins around it. "What difference does it make how I heard? What matters is that it didn't come from you. And you weren't going to tell me again, were you?"

Why did doing something right make him feel so guilty? "I was going to get around to it."

"When?" she demanded hotly. "After you'd been gone a week? A month? A year? But then, disappearing is your style, isn't it? I'm surprised you stayed this long."

He wanted to go to her, to hold her. To tell her that it wasn't his choice, but it was the one he had to make.

He remained where he was, because touching her would negate everything. Would make him stay when he needed to go. "It'll be better for everyone all around if I left."

"Everyone?" she echoed incredulously. "Who's everyone? It can't be the kids, because the whole town thinks you're the best pediatrician they've ever seen. And it certainly can't be me because I never wanted you to leave in the first place."

He felt so damn weary. With all his heart, he cursed his father's soul. "That's just it, I am doing this for you."

Hannah stared at him, stunned. "Me? How are you doing it for me?" Suddenly aware that she was shouting, she lowered her voice. "Did I ask you to go?"

If anything, everything about her had asked him to remain. But it didn't change the fact that he couldn't stay. Shouldn't stay. "It's better this way, you'll see."

How could he say that? How could he possibly *think* that? "No, I won't."

Allowing himself a single contact, he reached for her hand, but she pulled it away. He sought her eyes instead. "Trust me."

That was just it, she had. She'd sworn to herself that she wouldn't, not after the last time, after he'd disappeared on her like that, but she had. She had trusted him with her heart and now look where it had gotten her.

She shook her head, her voice as hollow as her soul felt right at this moment. "I doubt if I can. Ever again. I was beginning to, but now that's gone." Her eyes were accusing. "Just like you'll be."

Why was she making this so hard for him? Didn't she know how he felt about her? How he'd always felt? Couldn't she sense it? "Didn't you hear me? I'm doing this for you."

He was insulting her with a lie. Hannah fisted her hands in her lap. "Oh please, spare me. Spare me that at least. That old chestnut's as overused as—" her voice took on a martyr-like quality as she rolled her eyes heavenward "—'If it would have been anyone, it would have been you.'"

His face was somber as he looked at her. "It would have been. Is." If he could have taken that leap of faith for anyone, he would have taken it for her. Because he'd never loved anyone but her.

She didn't know whether to laugh or cry. "Words, Jackson, just empty words."

Unable to remain calm any longer, Jackson rose to his feet. "Damn it, do you think it's easy for me, leaving you?"

"Well, it must be, because you're doing it," she

shot back. "As fast as that expensive car of yours can go."

Jackson dug his knuckles into the blotter on his desk as he leaned over it, his face inches away from hers. "I'm doing it, damn it, because if I stayed, then I might do something stupid."

She rose too, facing him down. "Like what, Jackson? Like make love with me? Is that what you think is stupid?" She wanted to know. "Or are you afraid of suddenly feeling—what?" She thought of Ethan, of why he had gone out of his way to find and bed other women. Because she had disappointed him in bed. There was no other explanation for it. She couldn't find fault in any other part of the life they shared. It had to be that. "Noble intentions mingled with acute disappointment? Is that what has you running out of town?"

"What the hell are you talking about?" he asked.

"I'm talking about you running from me."

How much could he tell her without telling her everything? She had to be made to understand that the choice wasn't his to make. It had been preordained—if she were going to be happy. And above all, he wanted her to be happy.

"Don't you understand? I'm running from you because I can't stop thinking about you, because every time I see you, I want you. Because I want to make you my wife."

No, she didn't understand, she thought. And she was understanding less with each passing moment. "And this is what...repulsive to you?" Hannah fought back tears. "You think you're insane for wanting me?"

Helpless, he took her hands in his, then dropped them as if they were both on fire. He began to pace the room. "I'm insane *from* wanting you. Don't you understand? I can't do that to you."

"Now I'm the one completely lost. Do what to me?" Hannah asked.

Exasperation filled his voice. "Marry you."

She waited, but nothing more came in the wake of the declaration. "I'm still lost."

He said it as simply as he could. "I don't want to hurt you."

"And you think leaving isn't going to accomplish that?"

Jackson shook his head sadly. "Not as much as staying. As marrying you."

"Jackson, what are you talking about?" She wasn't going to leave here, she swore to herself, without getting this cleared up at least to her satisfaction. If she was going to be rejected a second time in her life, she was damn well going to know why. "Why would marrying you hurt me? Do you turn into a werewolf at the first sign of a full moon? I promise I won't arm myself with silver bullets," she said, sarcastically.

"What I would turn into," he said quietly, "would be something a great deal worse than a werewolf."

Now he was scaring her. Not with hints at creatures, but at what he believed existed inside of him. "What?" she wanted to know. "What could you possibly turn into that's worse than a werewolf?"

Turning away, he closed his eyes and gave her the rest of it. "I could turn into my father."

She stared at his back, waiting for him to turn

around. When he didn't, she moved around him until she was facing Jackson. "Excuse me?"

"My father," he repeated. "Jackson Caldwell, Sr., a man who was dedicated to the constant quest of conquering the next beautiful woman who came down the pike, all the while breaking the heart of a woman whose feet he wasn't fit to kiss."

She remembered what Gertie had told her, but couldn't see the connection between father and son, other than blood. They were nothing alike. Searching Jackson's face, she saw that he seemed to believe otherwise. "You're serious. You're leaving town, leaving me, because you think you're going to turn into a lecher?" It didn't make sense to her.

"Not a lecher, my father." He laughed shortly. "Although the two are synonymous."

How could he possibly believe what he was saying? Unless he was leading some double life she knew nothing about, and that simply wasn't possible in Storkville, there was no evidence for him to even begin to think he could be anything like his father.

"My God, Jackson, is that why—why—wow." She sank down in the chair, stunned by the revelation of what had been going on in his head all this time. "Is that what you think? That after a lifetime of being a good, kind and decent human being, you were suddenly going to grow fangs, bay at the moon and go tomcatting around, as Gertie likes to put it?" It stole her breath away. Pieces were beginning to fall together. "And here I thought—I thought—"

Jackson looked at her. "Thought what?"

She blinked, attempting to reconcile things in her

mind. "I thought that you pushed me toward Ethan because you didn't want me."

He laughed at the absurdity of that. "I pushed you toward Ethan because I wanted you, but I thought he could be everything for you that I couldn't be."

And that was the irony of it, she thought. "He was. He was fast, loose and as shallow as a two-year-old's wading pool. And completely engaged in making adultery his full-time hobby. Everything you weren't."

He was his father's son and the roots ran deep. "How can you be so sure?"

Pity filled her for what he had lived with. And anger with it for what he had made them both live. "Because I apparently know you a great deal better than you know yourself. Do you think this is genetic? Something that suddenly kicks in at a certain age?" She couldn't hold back the anger even though she tried. So many years wasted. So much misunderstanding. "Or maybe there's a switch inside that just turns on after you say 'I do' and then you don't want to? That was your father's style and Ethan's, not yours, Jackson."

His eyes told her she wasn't getting through. Her frustration mounted. "Look at you, look at your life. Everything your father was, you're not, other than good-looking and rich. Your father was ruthless, you're selfless." She jabbed a finger at his chest, at his heart. "Right there, that's the proof. You were always monogamous in your relationships." She drew a deep breath, remembering. "All of which I was incredibly jealous of."

He remembered going through the motions, trying

to deny his feelings for her, to sublimate them and scatter them to the winds by seeing other girls. It hadn't worked. "There was no reason to be. Those women meant nothing to me."

She was glad to hear it, even now. "That reinforces my point even more. You didn't care about them, and you still only dated one at a time."

He shoved his hands into his pockets, looking away. "I was trying not to be like my father."

"Well, guess what? You succeeded." Hannah stared at his back which was so stiff, so formal. She felt him drifting away from her and there was nothing she could do. The frustration clawed at her. "What makes you think that you can't continue not being your father?"

"The stakes are too high to risk finding out," he said.

And that would be her, Hannah thought. "Why don't you leave that for the stakes to decide?"

Jackson shook his head. "I won't risk it," he repeated.

Hannah looked at him in silence for a long moment. The emptiness within her grew to astounding portions. "You might not be like your father, but you're just like Ethan. Neither one of you thought I was good enough to stay with."

"That's not true." He reached for her, but she backed away, her eyes accusing.

"Isn't it?" she demanded hotly. "Ethan was always looking for something better, never giving me a chance to be that something better for him. And you, you're even worse, you won't even sample the goods before making up your mind."

His eyes were as dark as his soul felt. He was sending away the only thing in his life that mattered. "It's not about sex, Hannah."

Hannah pressed her lips together, fighting for control. "Well, it certainly isn't about love, is it? Because people who love each other try anything and everything they can to save what they have and more importantly, what could be." Something tore within her. She'd had enough. "You know what? You can just pack up your shingle and go, I don't care anymore. I'm through caring."

She crossed quickly to the door, then stopped, her hand on the knob. Hannah looked at him over her shoulder. "And I was wrong. You are like your father. Not because you'd be unfaithful but because you're completely heartless."

The door slammed in her wake.

The next few days were wrapped in a thick haze, moving around her like heavy smog. Hannah went through the motions, doing what was required of her, pushing ahead because it was the only thing that convinced her she was still alive, still breathing.

It amazed her how long a person could keep moving after their heart had been reduced to shattered pieces.

The others at the center noticed and tried their best not to appear as if they had. It was impossible not to detect that the spirit had left her voice, the zest had left her eyes. But she was trying. Trying very hard.

And for their parts, Gertie, Penny Sue and Gwenyth were incredibly cheerful, mentioning no topics heavier than the selection of the afternoon snack. She blessed them for it, blessed them for not asking, not trying to help a situation that was beyond mending.

The only thing that would do any good was time. And she would have plenty of that. Alone, she mused as she stood in the room she'd converted to the downstairs nursery, changing Steffie.

"Don't get mixed up with men, Steffie," she told the small, round face beaming up at her. "It's not worth the hassle."

"You're right."

Startled, she looked up and saw Jackson standing in her doorway. Something pulled within her stomach, tight and hard. He hadn't been by, on any pretext, for the last few days. She hadn't attempted to see him, steeling herself for a time when she wouldn't be able to see him.

He's come to say good-bye, she thought.

Closing the diaper, she picked Steffie up and tried to act as if her heart wasn't about to beat right out of her chest. "Which part?"

There were hints of circles under her eyes. She hadn't been sleeping. That made two of them, he thought.

Like a man testing icy waters, he slowly entered the room. "Take your pick."

"I'm through picking, through hoping."

He tried to get a better view of her face, to read her expression. "God, I hope not."

She placed Steffie back in the playpen in the next room. It was after hours. Penny Sue and Rebecca were gone, as were the children. Gertie had already said good-bye. Hannah assumed she must have let

Jackson in on her way out. Gwenyth was at her new place for the night.

"Why?" With effort, she kept her voice sufficiently without emotion. "What do you care?" The front room looked as if a tornado had gone through it. Because she had to keep busy, Hannah began picking up toys and putting them away. "Have you found a replacement yet?"

Getting down on his knees beside her, he started picking up pieces of a puzzle, placing them back into their frame. "I stopped looking."

She froze and looked at him. "Does that mean you're going to stay?"

His eyes met hers. Was it too late, he wondered. "Depends."

Don't, don't start hoping, Hannah, you know what happens when you start hoping. "On what?"

Tossing the puzzle piece he was holding aside, Jackson took her hands in his and slowly rose to his feet, bringing her up with him. "On whether I can get you to forgive me."

A smile flirted with her lips. "Which part?" she repeated.

He hadn't even been able to practice this. There was no right way to say it, so he just plunged in. "All of it. I've been a jerk…"

The smile became an easy grin. "Go on, so far we're in agreement."

He began to hope that it was going to be all right. That it wasn't too late to make amends and start over. "I've been running scared from my father's shadow for so long, I was doing exactly the very thing I didn't want to do. I was hurting you. I sent you into Ethan's arms and let him hurt you.''

The anger in her heart left as if it had never been there. ''It's not as if you had a crystal ball.''

She'd always been quick to forgive, he thought, but he wasn't. Not when it came to himself. ''No, but maybe if I'd had a little more faith in the man I could be…''

Her eyes smiled at him. ''I had faith enough for the two of us.''

''Had.'' He caught the single world that could wound him. ''Does that mean—?''

Because her heart was moved, she kissed his cheek. ''It means I made a reference to the past and used correct grammar. It doesn't mean that the feeling, or the faith, is gone.''

He took the plunge. ''So would you be willing to marry me?''

Her mouth dropped open, but recovery was quick. ''Only one way to find out.''

He held his breath. ''And that is?''

She was trying very hard to keep a straight face when everything inside her was cheering. ''Ask me.''

Taking her hands in his again, he looked into her eyes. ''Hannah, will you marry me?''

She drew her hands away, placing one on her heart. She fluttered her lashes. ''Oh Jackson, this is so sudden. I'm going to have to think about it.'' She turned away. The next second, she'd gone a full 360 degrees and was facing him again. ''I've thought about it. The answer's yes.'' Relief and joy flooded her as she threw her arms around him. ''It's always been yes.''

Sammy's babbling grew louder, drawing her attention away from Jackson momentarily. She still had responsibilities to think of. "What about the twins? I've gotten very attached to them. I can't just give them up unless we find their parents. You'd be taking on a wife and a ready-made family."

"Couldn't be better." His eyes washed over her face as he allowed the love he felt for her to finally emerge unshackled and unrestrained. "I don't deserve you."

She grinned. "True, but we'll work on that."

His arms closed around her as he drew her close to him. "Got a schedule worked out?"

"I thought we'd start immediately."

"Sounds good to me." How had he ever thought he could walk away from her again? Once had been hard enough, twice would have been impossible. "I love you Hannah."

She closed her eyes, savoring the sound. "Say it again."

"I love you, Hannah," he whispered. "I love you. I'll say it as often as you like and as often as it takes to convince you."

Mischief rose in her eyes. "You know what they say."

He laughed. "No, what do they say?"

She cocked her head. "Actions speak louder than words."

"I can do action," he murmured, his lips a scant inch from hers.

"I was counting on it." It was the last thing she said for quite some time.

*   *   *   *   *

Don't miss

HIS EXPECTANT NEIGHBOR

by
Teresa Southwick,

next month's installment of
STORKVILLE, USA, *coming to you*
from Silhouette Romance in
September 2000.

For a sneak preview,
please turn the page.

"Aw damn!" Sioux rancher Ben Crowe brought his truck to a screeching halt on the old dirt road that led to his home, shoved open the door and jumped out, nine-year-old Nathan Eastman on his heels. "I knew something like this was going to happen!"

Ben was a tall man, at least six feet. When he reached the very pregnant Gwenyth Parker, who was dragging a huge box up the steps of the cottage he'd rented to her only two days before, he towered over her. "What in the hell do you think you're doing?"

Because he was angry, and his voice dripped with it, he was surprised when she looked up and smiled. "I bought a walker for the baby," she said simply, her hazel eyes sparkling with joy.

Ben had heard all about the glow of pregnant women, but he had to admit this was the first time he'd actually seen it. Her eyes were so bright and her face was so radiant she could have lit the darkest night.

"No kidding," Ben said, scooping the unwieldy cardboard box out of her arms and carrying it up the steps. "Don't you know you're not supposed to be lifting heavy things?"

"It's not heavy," Gwen replied, her smile in place, her beautiful blond hair reflecting the rays of the early September sun. "Who's your friend?"

"That's Nathan," Ben said, unlocking her front door because, as her landlord, he had a key. "Don't change the subject. I rented this property to you on the condition that you'd be a good tenant."

"I am a good tenant," she said, right behind him as he set the big box on the floor beside her kitchen table. When he turned around, she was directly in front of him.

Dressed in simple jeans, maternity T-shirt and a bright blue sweater coat that wasn't designed for a woman in her seventh month and didn't button over her tummy, with her wind-blown shoulder-length hair tucked behind her ears, Gwenyth Parker was still impossibly beautiful, and Ben realized he could have stared at her lovely face all day.

It had been a long time since a woman stirred his senses. Because Gwen did, he took a step back, then shifted around her to go outside.

"Are there any more boxes in your car?"

She shrugged. "A few. But really, Ben. I didn't buy anything I couldn't carry myself."

He grunted an unintelligible response to that, then hurried out the door and down the steps to her car. He didn't know much about the newest resident of

Storkville, Nebraska, except that she was pregnant and she had divorced her husband, the baby's father, before she moved here. That was the first reason he'd been reluctant to rent the roadside cottage to her. He couldn't understand or condone a woman raising a baby alone when she had a perfectly good husband. The second reason was that he was afraid he would somehow become responsible for her. She had assured him he wouldn't, but in only a couple of days he was already carrying boxes.

"Where do you want these?" he asked, stepping into the kitchen again.

She pointed to the sofa in the small living room off to the right. "In there is good."

He gave her a patient look. "And how do you plan to get these up the stairs?"

Ben saw her pause, taking note of dark-haired Nathan, who still wore his good jeans and T-shirt from school and was behind Ben, more or less peeking around his waist at Gwen.

"Nathan," she said, "why don't you go out to the car and make sure there aren't any packages left?"

From the formal tone of her voice, Ben could tell her good mood was gone. Nathan must have sensed it too, because he didn't say anything, only grinned and nodded, then darted out of the house.

"Look, Mr. Crowe," she said coolly, her once-smiling face now drawn in anger. "I'm pregnant, not sick. I'm perfectly capable of taking care of myself."

"I'm sure you are," Ben agreed, not quite understanding how a sweet disposition could go sour in the blink of an eye, but glad to have her mention the issue that troubled him about her. Since she'd brought up this subject, he felt permitted to pursue it. "Is that why you left your husband? To prove you could take care of yourself? Because if it is, you should be ashamed of yourself. Babies need two parents."

He hadn't expected her angry face to fall in dismay, but it did. He'd driven her from unreasonably happy, to angry, to sad, so rapidly Ben immediately knew dealing with pregnant women wasn't his forte. He also knew he'd made a big mistake.

Quiet, stricken, Gwen said, "I think babies need two parents, too, but it wasn't my decision to get a divorce. It was my ex-husband's. If the choice had been mine, I would have raised my child with its father." With that she walked to the door. "If you don't mind, I have to put all this stuff away," she said, more than hinting that Ben should leave.

Confused because he was now more curious about her than before, but equally embarrassed because he'd upset her, he ran his hand across the back of his neck. Having been raised in foster homes, he understood the urge to confront her about not putting the welfare of her child first. Normally he had enough sense to stop himself from butting in if a problem wasn't any of his business. And since her first marriage, her first husband and even this baby weren't any of his business, it puzzled him that he hadn't thought this the whole way through before he'd opened his big mouth.

"I'm sorry," he apologized contritely. "I didn't mean to be so blunt, but when it comes to kids I know I'm overly protective since my own parents abandoned me."

With a brief nod, she more or less conceded that she understood what he'd said, but Ben knew it was too late. Not only had he stuck his foot in his mouth, but he'd also hurt her.

Walking to his truck, he felt like a real idiot. A blockhead, too stupid to tread lightly with a woman who had enough to deal with without having to listen to his criticism. He shouldn't have challenged her the way he had, but he quickly forgave himself because he truly was a person who cared about kids. Asking her that question, no matter how inappropriate, was second nature to him. So that took care of forgiving himself. Now, all he had to do was figure out how he could get *her* to forgive him....

If you enjoyed what you just read,
then we've got an offer you can't resist!

Take 2 bestselling love stories FREE!

Plus get a FREE surprise gift!

Clip this page and mail it to Silhouette Reader Service™

IN U.S.A.	IN CANADA
3010 Walden Ave.	P.O. Box 609
P.O. Box 1867	Fort Erie, Ontario
Buffalo, N.Y. 14240-1867	L2A 5X3

YES! Please send me 2 free Silhouette Romance® novels and my free surprise gift. Then send me 6 brand-new novels every month, which I will receive months before they're available in stores. In the U.S.A., bill me at the bargain price of $2.90 plus 25¢ delivery per book and applicable sales tax, if any*. In Canada, bill me at the bargain price of $3.25 plus 25¢ delivery per book and applicable taxes**. That's the complete price and a savings of at least 10% off the cover prices—what a great deal! I understand that accepting the 2 free books and gift places me under no obligation ever to buy any books. I can always return a shipment and cancel at any time. Even if I never buy another book from Silhouette, the 2 free books and gift are mine to keep forever. So why not take us up on our invitation. You'll be glad you did!

215 SEN C24Q
315 SEN C24R

Name	(PLEASE PRINT)	
Address	Apt.#	
City	State/Prov.	Zip/Postal Code

* Terms and prices subject to change without notice. Sales tax applicable in N.Y.
** Canadian residents will be charged applicable provincial taxes and GST.
   All orders subject to approval. Offer limited to one per household.
   ® are registered trademarks of Harlequin Enterprises Limited.

SROM00_R   ©1998 Harlequin Enterprises Limited

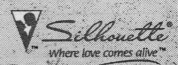

**Don't miss
an exciting opportunity
to save on the purchase of
Harlequin and Silhouette books!**

Buy any two Harlequin or
Silhouette books and save
$10.00 off future Harlequin
and Silhouette purchases

OR

buy any three
Harlequin or Silhouette books
and save **$20.00 off** future
Harlequin and Silhouette purchases.

*Watch for details
coming in October 2000!*

PHQ400

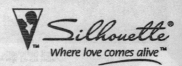

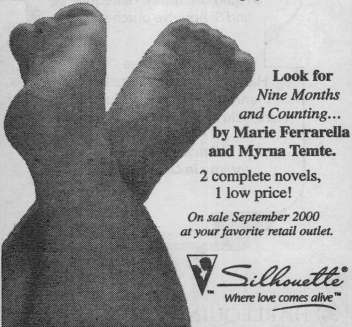

COMING NEXT MONTH

#1468 HIS EXPECTANT NEIGHBOR—Susan Meier
Storkville, USA
The *last* thing loner Ben Crowe wanted was a beautiful single
woman renting the cottage on his ranch—and a pregnant one at
that! Yet when Gwen Parker gave him her sweet smile, how could
he refuse? And how could he guard his hardened heart?

#1469 MARRYING MADDY—Kasey Michaels
The Chandlers Request...
It was one week before Maddy Chandler's wedding to a safe,
sensible man, and she should have been ecstatic. But then her
former love Joe O'Malley suddenly moved in right next door,
with plans to show lovely Maddy *he* was the groom for her!

#1470 DADDY IN DRESS BLUES—Cathie Linz
When Curt Blackwell went to check out his daughter's new
preschool, he was surprised to find that her enticing teacher,
Jessica Moore, was "Jessie the Brain" from their high school days!
Suddenly Curt was looking forward to staying after school....

#1471 THE PRINCESS'S PROPOSAL—Valerie Parv
The Carramer Crown
Brains, beauty...a prize stallion—Princess Adrienne de Marigny
had Hugh Jordan's every desire. And he had a little something *she*
wanted. The princess's proposal involved a competition, winner
take all. But the plan backfired, leading to a different proposal....

#1472 A GLEAM IN HIS EYE—Terry Essig
Johanna Durbin was on her own after helping raise her siblings—
and intended to enjoy single life. That is, until she met sexy
guardian Hunter Pace, who needed daddy lessons—fast! But was
Hunter looking for a temporary stint...or a family forever?

#1473 THE LIBRARIAN'S SECRET WISH—Carol Grace
Tough, brooding, calloused—and devilishly handsome—
investigator Nate Callahan was the kind of guy librarian
Claire Cooper had learned to stay away from. Still, how could
she turn her back on a missing little boy? Or on a chance to feel
the love she'd always dreamed of...?

CMN0800